MW01386022

Time Travel at Jagged Rock Lighthouse

Time Travel at Jagged Rock Lighthouse

Nancy Bayne

A DIVISION OF THOMAS NELSON

WestBow Press books may be ordered through booksellers or by contacting:

WestBow Press
A Division of Thomas Nelson
1663 Liberty Drive
Bloomington, IN 47403
www.westbowpress.com
1-(866) 928-1240

ISBN: 978-1-4497-7857-6 (e)
ISBN: 978-1-4497-7858-3 (sc)
ISBN: 978-1-4497-7856-9 (hc)

Library of Congress Control Number: 2012923011

Printed in the United States of America

WestBow Press rev. date: 12/27/2012

To Tim and Lauren
who believed in me

CONTENTS

Preface

I was inspired to write this story when I visited Split Rock Lighthouse in Two Harbors, Minnesota. I stood where the first lightkeeper stood and wondered what it would have been like to live there. I visited nineteen more lighthouses after that. Jagged Rock Lighthouse is made up of all the lighthouses I saw and read about. If you want to learn more about real lighthouses, go to www.mnhs.org.

Acknowledgments

I'd like to thank my husband for his encouragement and my daughter for her review and suggestions on the manuscript. Joe Elliott did an excellent job of proofreading the earlier drafts. Thanks to Cassie Frohberg for her help with photos. Jenny Gegg took the author photograph and was very helpful. The Lincoln-area writers' group patiently listened to the story as I read it aloud, and the members' critiques made it a much better book. I'd like to thank the Minnesota Historical Society for all of its helpful information on Split Rock Lighthouse and lighthouses in general.

Chapter 1:

A Flash

"There it is!" I yelled as the lighthouse popped up through the trees. In my enthusiasm, I forgot no one would care.

"Don't yell, Paige," said my stepmother. "You're giving me a headache."

"Dad, don't you want to see it? It's really famous."

Dad didn't answer. My stepmother answered for him. "No, not really," she said as she rubbed sunscreen on her face. "Your dad and I are going hiking."

"We're going fishing," my "dear" brother Joshua said with a sneer.

I realized then that they were going to drop me off at the lighthouse and go about their merry way.

"Isn't it illegal to leave a minor alone in a state park?" I didn't know, but I was mad. I had a cell phone, but I didn't know if I would get good reception.

"Don't be ridiculous, Paige," my stepmother snapped. "What could possibly happen?"

I didn't say anything because I didn't really know.

"She thinks someone will abduct her because she's so beautiful," Jared, my other ten-year-old twin brother, said.

No one scolded him or even commented.

I was a little worried about that very thing. I read a lot and knew it happened. But I really wanted to see the lighthouse.

I wanted to shoot some great photographs to post on a photography Internet site. My mom and I used to read books together about lighthouses, and I had always dreamed of seeing a real one.

So I steeled myself to go alone. *At least I'll have Maggie.* I patted our chocolate Labrador. My dad pulled the van up to the curb.

"What are you waiting for? Get out!" My stepmother yanked the door open and turned away from me.

So without looking at my silent dad, I grabbed my camera and the dog leash and got out. "Come, Maggie!" The Lab leaped over the seat onto the concrete and turned around expectantly.

"Here. Closing time," my stepmother said. The door slammed and they drove away.

I watched the van, even after the green rectangle turned right and slipped behind the trees that lined the Minnesota highway. I had a tiny hope they would change their minds. I knew it wasn't going to happen, but I still stood rooted to the curb. Tears threatened to erupt.

This made me mad. I hate crying. It never does any good, and you end up looking like a swollen lobster. Anger is much more useful.

"Oh, blow them," I said as I stomped up and down the sidewalk, swiping my bangs from my eyes. I decided this was a waste of time. "Come on, Maggie. Let's go see a lighthouse."

We sprinted toward the entrance, my camera tucked in my pocket. I paid the fee, took several steps forward, and saw the top of the yellow tower spiking through the trees. "Whoa!" I stopped abruptly. Maggie ran into the back of me, jabbing me with her cold nose.

We walked farther, gaining a clear view of the whole lighthouse. Jagged Rock Lighthouse stood on a hundred-foot cliff and rose, castlelike, into a sunny sky.

"Sweet," I said to Maggie. She barked and wagged her tail. Maggie always agreed with whatever I said, which is why I love dogs, especially Maggie. "Time for some serious photography."

I babysat the very rowdy Martin toddlers every week. I had saved up enough money to buy a good camera. I had studied a photographer, Dorothea Lange, who had taken a lot of famous photographs during the Depression. I wished to buy a camera that used film, just like Dorothea had, but film was too expensive, so I settled for digital. I wanted to capture beauty on my camera. There wasn't a whole lot of that in my life.

Maggie and I got to work.

I walked around the lighthouse and shot photos from every vantage point: far away, close up, on the right, on the left, in the middle. I climbed some boulders to get a higher view until someone yelled at me to get down. I lay on the sidewalk for a picture of the tower, which gave it a tall, ominous look. Maggie kept trying to lick my face.

Time to climb up to the top of the lighthouse. We trotted over to the lightkeeper's office, which was connected to the lighthouse. I was ready to dash inside, only to be called back by a guide's screechy voice. "You can't go up yet. It's full of people."

I sighed as I stepped back. I like things to happen right now. Instead we walked to the cliff's edge. "Whoa," I said. A hundred-foot drop into Lake Superior. Luckily, a chain-link fence protected us from falling. Maggie put her front paws on the top of the fence and wagged her tail.

The water stretched as far as I could see. No land in sight. The sun danced off the water. A slight breeze tickled my hair.

But I wanted to see the lighthouse. I turned around and walked back to the entrance. Tired of waiting, I butted my way through the crowd. I'm not small and neither is my dog. I kept stepping on people's feet, and Maggie tickled their legs. Good thing the guide faced the other direction. Somehow Maggie and I managed to shove our way into the lightkeeper's office.

"We have restored this room to what it was like when it opened in 1910," said a male guide, who was wearing a lighthouse keeper's uniform. It looked military, with navy pants and a jacket with brass buttons. The blue hat with a brim sported a lighthouse insignia, the patch of the U.S. Lighthouse Service, we learned from the guide. Bodies pressed against each other, and the smell of sweat wafted in the air. Stifling. No cool breeze like outside. To reach the top of the lighthouse, I'd have to endure the crowd.

I could see a wood-burning stove in the corner near a desk. On the desk were a kerosene lantern, some maps and charts, the lightkeeper's journal, and his hat. It looked like he had just left and would be back any minute.

I'm standing right where the lightkeeper did in 1910. In my mind, I could see him working away in the tower, lighting the lamps to make sure ships didn't crash into the rocks. *What was his name? Did he have any children? Why did he become a lighthouse keeper?*

"Lake Superior is the largest freshwater lake in the world," the guide boomed.

I shot a picture while the female guide brought in a new group, making it even more crowded. "This is the authentic journal of the lightkeeper," she said. Her shrill voice hurt my ears. I raised my camera to take a picture of the journal. I stood too close, took a step backward, and stumbled on a person behind me. Now someone's arm swung in the way. I ducked down—a good angle, but the journal sat too far to the left. I reached out to scoot the journal over and touched it. The screechy guide said, "Don't handle the journal!"

Flash! An empty room! I straightened up and looked around. I heard a fire crackling in the wood stove; there hadn't been one before. The smell of sweat was gone. Everything else looked exactly the same.

Where did everyone go? Am I going crazy?

CHAPTER 2:

Mr. Whisker Man

HEAVY BOOTS CLUNKED DOWN THE tower steps.

A man appeared, dressed like the other guides, in the same uniform and hat, except that he had the most extraordinary whiskers, long and bushy, sprouting from his chin. They covered his mouth and cascaded down his chest. Maggie trotted right up to him while I held back.

He looked surprised. "Well, now, Miss Beauty, where'd you come from?" He bent over to scratch her ears. "Did Ralph bring you 'round to play?"

"Her name is Maggie," I began.

The guide stood up, hitting his head on the railing, and sat down hard on the floor, his hat falling off. "Ouch," he said, rubbing his head.

I ran over. "I'm sorry. I didn't mean to startle you. Are you all right?" I stood there like a helpless idiot.

He just sat there.

I hoped he didn't have a concussion. I kept quiet to be polite, but I couldn't help blurting out, "Are those whiskers real?"

The man looked up. I babbled on. "I'm sorry. It's just that I don't know anyone with a beard like yours. And where did all of the visitors go? This room was full a minute ago." I looked at him expectantly.

He finally recovered his voice, but ignored my questions. "You scared the living daylights out of me. Did your dory get blown off course?" His eyes narrowed. "Who are you? Are you a ghost?"

I snorted. "No. Are you?"

"No," he said, rubbing his head. And then he looked me square in the eyes. "Ghost or no, young people need to be respectful. Now help me up."

This shut me up. I grabbed his beefy hand and tugged. Finally he heaved to his feet.

He looked down at my tennis shoes with interest. "Really … what are those contraptions on your feet? I never seen any shoes like that before." Then he looked at me again and his face turned bright red. "Why are you wearing only your undergarments?" He turned his face away as he asked this. "You're practically naked." Only he said it like *neck-ed*.

I glanced down at my shorts and cami. My underwear wasn't showing. "What do you mean?"

"Where are your clothes? Maybe you got a bump on the head." He unbuttoned his wool coat. "Here. Put this on brisklike. We can't have you running around like *that*."

I sympathized with Alice in Wonderland.

What is happening? Why would a guide be so weird? I didn't know what he meant, but I put on his itchy jacket while he turned his back.

"Let's take this slow," the man said, stroking his mustache with his thumb and index finger. "My brain is getting all stirred up and I can't think proper." We both sat down in high-backed wooden chairs.

"I'm the keeper here, Nels Christiansen. And your name?"

"Paige Johnson."

"Good Scandinavian name. Who's this fine animal?"

"Maggie." Maggie had been wiggling, just waiting to be noticed again. Nels gave her a pat on the head and looked at me.

"What in blazes are you doing in my lighthouse?"

"I came here to take pictures. See? Here's my camera." I showed him, but it increased his confusion.

"Never seen one like that before. Is your boat moored good and tight?"

"I don't have a boat ..." I tapped my foot. "We drove here. From Nebraska."

"A horse?"

Is this man nuts? "Of course not. In a van."

"What's a van?"

"Umm, you drive it. On a road. Ours is a Ford." I couldn't help a little sarcasm creeping into my voice.

"A Ford? You mean one of them automobiles?" His eyes narrowed. "Boats are it," he said. "No road goes here. No other people. I'm the first keeper and we just opened." He patted the wall lovingly.

"Just opened?"

"Yes. I remember I was so anxious, I lit the light the night before I was supposed to. We rowed out in the boat just to see her shinin'." He grabbed his suspenders, pulled them out, and snapped them for emphasis. "It was somethin'."

He expanded on this saga, but my brain stuck on two words: *just opened.* "You just opened the lighthouse?" The root of a horrible idea grew inside my head that explained where all of the people had gone.

"Yep, in May. She's the finest lighthouse you'll ever see."

"What year? What year?"

He finally heard me. "Nineteen ten. What's wrong? You've gone all palelike."

"You're not a guide?"

His face looked blank.

"What's today's date?" I asked. I broke out in a cold sweat.

"This here is June 15, 1910. I just wrote it in the journal." He walked to the desk and tapped the entry with his finger. I followed him and looked over his shoulder. My stomach did a nosedive. Sure enough, the entry said, "June 15, 1910."

CHAPTER 3:

Somewhere in Time

I SAT DOWN AND FORCED my head between my knees. My coach told us to do that if we felt faint. I tried to breathe. What can I say? I'm bravery personified.

Unfortunately, when I sat up, Mr. Whisker Man still waited there. I had hoped that my head had cracked open and that when I awoke from my delirium, he would have disappeared.

He scratched his mustache. "How 'bout if we have some coffee?" I put my head between my knees again. I heard the dribble of liquid. He tapped me on the shoulder and handed me a tin cup.

I didn't like coffee, but I took a sip anyway. It tasted hot and strong and speckled with grounds. The man pulled out his chair, swung it backward, and straddled it with his arms on top. He didn't speak while I sipped the liquid. The coffee felt soothing going down.

When I realized I was going to live, I said, "Thanks for the coffee. I'll try to answer your questions now."

"How old are you?"

"I'm twelve."

"Why are you turning the color of a mushroom's underbelly?"

"I'm not from here." The understatement of all time.

"I know. You said Nebraska."

"Yes, but …." *here goes:* "I live in a different year."

"What? You're right here in 1910."

"I know." My voice quavered.

He shook his head in disbelief. "I admit you have an outlandish look about you."

I whispered it because it seemed less fantastic. "I live in the twenty-first century. The new millennium and all that." My voice squeaked.

The keeper didn't say anything. Instead he took off his hat, turned it upside down, brushed off some lint, transferred the hat to the other hand, and then put it back on.

"That's quite a tale. I'll have to think on it. I've seen and heard a few unusual things in my life." He tugged at his earlobe and then looked down at his hands. "But," he insisted, "I was born in 1875. And this here is really 1910."

How could that be? I must be going crazy. Maggie put her front paws on my lap. I pushed her down, stood up, and walked to the window. I couldn't get over that it was the same lake, the same view. The only difference was the fence—there wasn't one.

"Does everyone in the future travel?"

"N—no …at least not that I know of."

The keeper continued to tug at his mustache. "How did you get here?"

I shrugged. "I don't know. I went to visit the lighthouse. I touched the journal and then something flashed. All the people disappeared. Then you thundered down the steps. Is that mustache real? I can't even see your mouth."

He laughed and twirled the ends of his marvelous mustache. "Sure is. Won a contest once. How does this here lighthouse look in the twenty-first century?"

"Very much like this. It's beautiful."

"Well, no matter what year you're from, I'd still like to show you 'round. Wanna see the lighthouse?"

"Yes!"

We walked over to the base of the tower. The stairs spiraled up in loops, hugging the walls. The spirals appeared to go on to infinity, like peering into a giant kaleidoscope.

The keeper led the way up the spiral staircase, forty-five feet into the sky. In my excitement to see the top, I forgot to take any photos. I started up, tennis shoes quiet on the metal steps. Maggie followed, her toenails clicking. I started to get dizzy, and Maggie whimpered more the higher we got. We slowed down, and I hugged the metal handrail. Eventually we made it.

Dotted with windows and full of light, the top smelled like sun on oak and fresh paint. As the sun shone on the magnifying lens, puddles of colored light danced everywhere. The floor was newly painted, the brass shone, the wooden window frames were polished, and the white brick walls were scrubbed clean. The gears that made the lens revolve constantly generated a click, click, click noise. The gear system resembled my gran's grandfather clock with its weights and pulleys. A sign said that the Fresnel lens was imported from Paris. It was worth the climb.

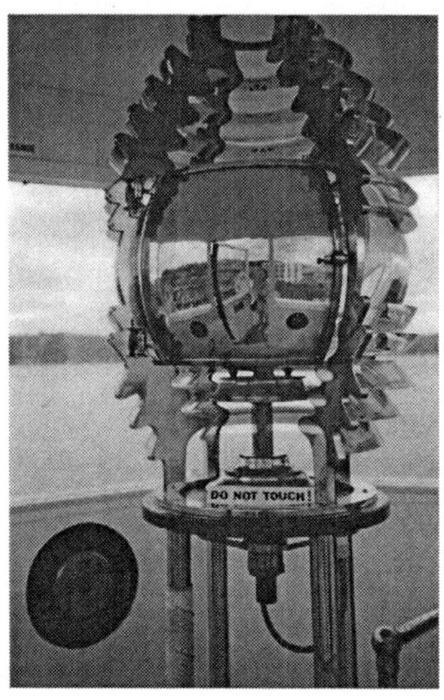

An example of a lighthouse lens.

I wanted a photo of that lens. I had read about them before I came. The lens contained little prisms. The overall shape reminded me of a beehive. The kerosene lanterns inside the hollow lens produced the light, and the lens gathered the light into a beam that shot into the night. The keeper explained how the lamps burned kerosene through a wick and said the kerosene had to be replenished before it ran out. The wicks had to be trimmed or the flame burned dangerously high.

We climbed up to the platform. I took more pictures. I wanted to climb the ladder to the catwalk, which led outside. *I could get great pictures out there.* I was so excited when the keeper motioned for me to climb up to see the lens more closely. "Now, be careful," he said. I shot some tight photos of the lens and its prisms.

"How far away can you see the light?" I asked.

"Twenty-two miles," he said, and snapped his suspenders. "Thirty miles on a clear night."

Night. This made me think about where I was. "Excuse me, but I should go home now," I said.

The idea of staying terrified me. *I'll just touch the journal and return to my time.*

He thrust out his hand. "Nice to meet you. How is the twenty-first century?"

I smiled. "It's pretty good!" I grabbed Maggie. We rushed downstairs. "Bye," I said, and placed my hand on top of the journal, just like before.

I closed my eyes. No flash.

I opened my eyes.

The keeper was looking at me. "Was somethin' supposed to happen?"

"Uh, yeah." I put my hand on the journal again. Nothing. I began to get another creepy feeling.

I grabbed the journal and opened it. All of the entries after 1910 had disappeared.

"What's wrong?" asked the keeper.

I whipped through page after page. They were all blank. I put my palm on every page, but I remained. I slammed my fist down on the book and it crashed to the floor.

I looked up at the keeper. "All of the pages from the future are gone."

"Is that bad?"

Monster hands of fear grabbed me. "I think it means I'm trapped in 1910."

CHAPTER 4:

Mrs. Keeper

I WAS SHAKING ALL OVER.

The keeper peered into my face. His eyebrows were raised in doubt. But he only voiced concern. "Now don't worry. You can stay with my family. I have two little girls, and I sure would want someone to take care of them if they got, er, lost. Why don't you come to the house? I can leave the lighthouse for a bit. It's a while before I have to light the lamp." He took my arm carefully and led me out.

We went into the house. "Let's go to the parlor," he said. "Here, sit on this fancy ladies' chair. I think it's called a fainting couch. You lie down on it. My wife insisted we have one. Sit down. I'll get my wife." He turned and yelled, "Ingrid! Ingrid! We have a visitor!"

He pushed open the swinging door to the kitchen and disappeared. I leaned back into the cushions of the funny chair. I refused to think of "the problem." It couldn't be true anyway. I would just sit and rest and block it from my mind. I closed my eyes. Maggie put her head on my leg.

I heard a swish. I opened my eyes, and a beautiful, blonde woman in a floor-length skirt was squinting down at me.

"Hello," she said. "Here is a cup of tea. It's soothing when you've had a shock." She held a china teacup in the air somewhere above my head. I sat up, managed to grab it without spilling the tea, and took a sip.

The woman gathered up her long skirts in one hand, felt with her other hand for the cushion of a chair, and sat down next to me.

"I am Ingrid Christiansen," she said. "I also brought some bread and jam that the children and I made." She put it on the table. "Nels is always rescuing people from boats, so I'm rather used to strangers popping up out of nowhere ... This is a new one, though." She wrinkled up her face. "I can't see you at all. I'm supposed to wear my spectacles all of the time but ... I like to meet people without them. For one brief moment, no spectacles."

She sighed and started patting her apron pockets. Finally, she found the right pocket, pulled out some wire-framed glasses, and put them on. They were quite thick. The change in her appearance was huge. Her eyes shrunk to tiny pools of blue, almost disappearing from her face. "I know, I know. I look like someone's great-granny. But let me have a good look at you."

She sized me up for a minute. "Are you really from the future?"

I choked up. "Yes," I said without bawling. "Are you Swedish?" I asked, guessing from her blonde hair.

"Ya," Ingrid said and laughed. It was a beautiful sound, like a bell ringing.

"I am, too," I said. "My great-grandparents emigrated from Helsingborg."

"Ah, your blonde hair and blue eyes gave you away. And what would your Swedish name be?"

"Johnson. Paige Johnson." I felt out of place next to this gorgeous creature with her swishing skirts and Cinderella hair. I couldn't think of anything to say.

In the silence I could hear a clock ticking. Then Ingrid spoke. "I hope you don't mind if I ask a question, but I'm so curious." She pointed at my shorts. "Is that what girls wear in the future?"

I nodded. I looked at Ingrid's voluminous skirts. I burst out, "Your outfit is much more beautiful!"

My jacket was knotted around my waist, and Ingrid reached out and touched it. "What's it made of?" she asked.

"It's microfiber."

Ingrid looked puzzled.

"I dunno. Plastic, I think. Someone invented it to be waterproof, breathable, lightweight, for hiking or sports." I could see none of this was clearing up Ingrid's confusion, so I looked at the tag. "Polyester, acrylic, nylon, and spandex."

"It's slippery," said Ingrid. "Do women wear trousers, too, or just girls?"

I thought of Gran, who loved to wear the loudest Bermuda shorts she could find, like ones with flamingos on them. "Women, too," I said.

"Ya? How nice!" Ingrid said and clapped her hands. "I shall look forward to that. I have often helped my husband at the lighthouse during a storm. These skirts get so heavy when they're wet. If I need to hurry, it's difficult. Many a time I have tripped and fallen in the mud. I tried Nels's overalls once, but they're so big! And then the lighthouse inspector arrived, and I had to hide behind the barn so he wouldn't see me!" She laughed. "That would have caused quite a stir."

"Why?"

"Oh, women in trousers, it's quite against regulations. So many regulations." She sighed. "We have surprise inspections. They look at the lighthouse *and* the house. I'm afraid I've put dirty dishes in the oven and laundry under the bed. It did *look* nice. We passed the inspection. I'm afraid Nels gets rather worked up and wishes I were tidier. But I'm straying from the subject."

Laughter pushed away my fears for a moment. "How many layers of skirt are you wearing under there?" I asked. This probably wasn't a polite question, but I wanted to know.

"Well, there's a skirt and several petticoats." She dropped her voice to a whisper. "And then pantaloons, you know."

"Pantaloons?"

"Bloomers. Really, my mother would be appalled that I'm discussing such things," she whispered.

I thought for a minute. "Oh! Underwear!"

After an enlightening discussion on women's fashions and enjoying tea, some bread, and jam, I quit shaking and felt a little better. "Thank you for the bread and tea," I said. "I'd better go back to the lighthouse." I stood up and put on the keeper's jacket. I wanted to try again to go home.

"Of course. Nels is up there. We must find you some clothes." She smiled at me. Not in that fake way that adults do when you have to go to grown-up gatherings. A real smile. "It's been a pleasure to meet you, Miss Johnson."

CHAPTER 5:

Disaster or Adventure?

As I STUMBLED OUT THE door, I tripped over Maggie. Sincerity like Ingrid's makes me nervous and clumsy. I'm not used to it. So does beauty. Cinderella gets gorgeous one day. No sign of that yet with me.

We walked to the keeper's office. I grabbed Maggie by the collar, just in case. I placed my hand flat down on the journal like before. I closed my eyes and then opened them. Nothing happened. I opened the journal and touched each page again. No flash.

Maggie's collar was twisting, turning my hand blue, so I let her flop on the floor. I turned the book upside down and touched each page again. I clutched the journal and walked to different parts of the office. I grabbed the window that opened to the vast lake. I stood next to the wood burning stove. I walked to the bottom of the steps. Still nothing happened.

"Arrgh!" I yelled in anger and waved a fist at the sky. Maggie hid under the desk, whimpering.

I stood in exactly the spot where I had been when I arrived. I touched everything in the room: the oil lamp, the navigational charts, the books, the window, the floor. I bent over, touched the floor with one palm and grasped the journal with the other, my butt in the air. Maggie kept sticking her nose into my face. I hurled the journal across the room in frustration.

I turned around and Nels was standing there. I jumped when I saw him. "Sorry." I picked up the journal and put it back on the desk. "I … was, uh, trying different things," I offered as an excuse.

He took a pipe out of his pocket. "If that journal's your means of gettin' home, you might want to take good care of it."

He didn't raise his voice, even though he obviously saw what I had done. He didn't even look mad. *Why isn't he angry?* At home I would have been in big trouble. His reaction made me so nervous I straightened the rest of the desk.

I looked up. He chewed on an unlit pipe and leaned against the brick wall.

"Sorry," I said. He nodded.

"How come you never light the pipe?" I said to change the subject.

"With gallons of kerosene everywhere? We'd blow ourselves sky high, right up to the pearly gates. I have some livin' I want to do first."

A picture of us floating up to heaven popped into my head. *It would be more like us in pieces,* I thought grimly. I shook my head to erase that image. "Unpleasant thought, I know." The keeper nodded. "Let's talk about something else. Tell me everything that happened up to coming here."

I couldn't tell if the keeper believed my story. He never displayed a whisper of doubt. I told the story in detail from the time we left the motel room until I arrived. He listened carefully.

"The journal is obviously the key," he said slowly. "What do you think the flash was?"

I felt more tired than I ever had in my life. "Of course it's the journal!" I burst out. "I touched the journal and I came here. How would I know what the flash was? This isn't supposed to be happening. It happens only in books. I want to go home!"

All during this tirade, the keeper just stared at me. He still didn't yell back. When I was done, he didn't say anything but continued to twirl his mustache. Finally he spoke.

"Why?" he asked.

"Why what?"

"Why do you want to go right home? Why are you in such a hurry?"

Stunned, I said, "Well, uh, I dunno. I live there."

"Well, you still do. Have you been away from home before?"

"Sure. Lots of times."

"Without your parents?"

"Yes."

"Are you really homesick?"

I thought about this. I wasn't *really* homesick. I shook my head no. "I just don't want anything to happen to my dad."

"Has he shown any penchant for time traveling?"

"Uh, no."

"My guess is that he's fine. You'll probably get back at the same day you left. Your family could be right where you left them. And you're possibly standing right here in the future." He pointed to the lighthouse floor.

This is a very odd idea. "You don't think my dad is in danger because I'm here?"

"No. He probably doesn't even know you're gone."

I sighed in relief. If my dad was okay, that made a big difference.

The keeper's voice interrupted my thoughts. "But what is it you're really afraid of?" he asked.

Is this twenty questions? Who's this guy anyway? But I realized what was really bothering me. "I'm afraid of not ever getting back to my time."

"Yes, I can see that," he said. "But I don't think this was random. How many hundreds of people must have touched that journal? Believe me, you're our only visitor from the future."

"Millions," I said.

"Millions?"

"Millions of visitors at the lighthouse. It's very popular."

The keeper grinned at this, a smile so big that I got the first glimpse of his straight, white teeth under the mustache. He whistled. "Well, I'll be. I knew we had a good one here. So we get famous, eh?"

I smiled. "Very."

"Can't wait to tell the wife. Where was I? Oh, you're the only one who's gotten here. I don't think you accidentally fell into some time hole. I think you came here for a reason. We just have to figure out what it is." He paused and winked at me. "Makes it kind of interesting, eh?"

I tried to look at it from that angle. I got a little glimpse and then it was gone. It felt odd, like a new shoe. "Then you think I'll be able to get back home?"

"Yes, I think you'll be able to get home when you accomplish whatever you're here for."

I sighed with relief. *It's an adventure. What is Gran always saying? Grab hold of life. Something like that. But I'm still going to touch the journal every day, just in case.*

CHAPTER 6:

An Emergency of Another Sort

I HAD TO GO TO the bathroom. I don't ever remember reading about a heroine like Cinderella needing to go "potty." But I couldn't put off this moment any longer. I was ready to burst.

"Thank you." Then I lowered my voice. "Where is your bathroom?"

"Oh, we don't have a bathroom. We take baths in a metal tub in the kitchen," said the keeper. "It's quite a production. Heating water and dumping it in. It takes all evening for everyone to get a bath."

People had to go to the bathroom here. "Where's your restroom?" I asked, blushing.

"Restroom?"

If I didn't speak up, there was going to be an accident. "I have to go number one."

The lightkeeper rubbed his whiskers. "Number one?"

"I need the john!" I blurted out in exasperation. "Toilet. Lavatory. Little girl's room." Politeness was lost in desperation.

Now it was the keeper's turn to be embarrassed.

"Oh, the privy. Sorry. Should have thought of that earlier. I got so interested in you being here. The privy is out back. It's a two-seater made of oak. Brought it over special, tied to a boat. It's a fine one. I'll show you."

I didn't know what a privy was, but I hoped it was what I needed. I was beginning not to care and looked for a suitable tree.

I followed the keeper behind the house. He pointed to a tiny shack. *Oh, an outhouse.* "Here it is. I'll wait over here for you." He withdrew behind a tree and began to whistle.

I pulled the rope handle on the door. A rancid smell slapped me in the face. I held my breath to avoid the odor and plunged into the dark shack. The daylight seeped in the corners. I thought about peering down the hole but decided against it. I did my business as quickly as possible. *If this is the finest privy, I would hate to see a bad one.* No toilet paper. Only catalogs. I got out fast, the door slamming behind me, and only then did I take a breath. Off the lake, the air was cool and crisp. I looked around for a sink to wash my hands.

The keeper appeared.

"I need to wash my hands."

"Really? Is that what you do in the future? The pump is over here."

We walked over to a metal thingy in the ground. The keeper pumped the handle and water gushed out. I stuck my hands under it. The water splattered all over me.

"Any soap?" I hollered. The keeper kept pumping. "Soap?" He looked around, as if soap would be hanging from a tree.

"My wife has some back at the house." I wiped my hands on the jacket tied around my waist. The keeper said, "It's time for supper." We headed to the house to face family dinner and what the kids thought of me, the sudden intruder.

CHAPTER 7:

Meet the Family

WHEN WE ARRIVED AT THE house, it wasn't quite time for dinner, so Ingrid led me to the guest room and pulled the door shut. I sank onto the bed, burrowed into the quilt, and drifted off.

Ingrid knocked on the door when it was time to eat. I inched out of bed and looked in the mirror, aghast at what I saw. I poured water into a bowl from a matching pitcher and washed my face. I didn't have a comb, so I removed the rubber band from my ponytail, smoothed the straggling hairs back in with my hand, and put my hair up again. My teeth were coated with fuzz, screaming for a toothbrush.

I opened a cabinet, basically snooping. A shaving brush and mug were perched inside. A metal rod that looked like a curling iron was also hidden in the cabinet. But no plug or cord dangled from the end, attesting to the lack of electricity. I finally I found a box labeled "Tooth Powder," and I sprinkled some on my finger and scrubbed my teeth. It was disgusting. I rinsed it out as fast as possible with a glass of water from the pitcher and spit into the bowl provided. I gave up on personal hygiene and headed to the kitchen.

"It smells wonderful," I said. One by one, blonde heads turned around to stare.

"These are my children," said Ingrid. She put her hand on the tallest head. "This is James, who is ten. This is Nellie, who is nine, and this is Sarah, who is five years old."

"I'm very pleased to meet you," I said. The children gawked at me like I was a green alien with antennae.

Sarah tugged on her mother's skirt. "Mommy, is she wearing her bloomers?" I glanced down at my shorts and then at the girls. I was wearing quite a bit less. I was getting rather weary of the references to my clothing.

"Honey, that's not very polite. She is our guest. We want to make her feel welcome."

"All right, Mommy." Sarah grabbed my hand and yanked me over to a chair. "You sit here." She patted the wooden stool. I sat down. "I picked the beans for you."

Meanwhile, Nellie and James were huddled in the corner, as if I couldn't hear them. "How did she get here?" hissed James.

"She must be an awfully good rower," whispered Nellie.

"There's no new boats at the dock."

"How *did* she get here?" asked Nellie.

"I don't know."

"Children, quit whispering and come here and sit down," said Ingrid in a stern voice as she put down a bowl of mashed potatoes.

Nellie and James took their places across from me, throwing suspicious glances my way. *I must have committed some 1910 felony.* I tried to ignore them by playing with my napkin.

"We're having a special dinner to welcome you," said Ingrid. She put out a basket of warm bread, the homemade kind. The scent filled the room.

"Thank you very much," I said. Nels arrived, removed his lightkeeper's hat, and hung it on a peg. Ingrid and Nels sat down.

They all held hands. Ingrid took my left hand, and Sarah's little hand grabbed my right one, including me in the family circle.

Nels blessed the food. "Lord, thank you for this food you have provided and the hand of my wife who prepared it. Thank you for the good weather. Help us to keep the light going so that there are no shipwrecks. Thank you for our guest who you sent to us. Help her to find her way home at the right time. Amen."

No one said much during the next few minutes, except for "Pass the chicken." I'd never had a better dinner in my life. Nellie and James kept stealing looks at me, but I ignored them.

After dinner and dishes, everyone gathered in the parlor. I picked a rocking chair in the corner, where I wanted to hide. I studied my fingernails, which were looking pretty good except for my index finger, which I had gnawed in the van.

The keeper sat down and tried to pull off his tall boots. I peered through my bangs. He couldn't bend his leg enough to get a good grip on them. I think his stomach was in the way. He kept snorting and huffing with each tug.

"Ingrid, my dear, could you give me a hand?"

Ingrid walked over to the keeper, and he stuck his booted foot in the air. She gripped the toe and sole and gave a small pull, but nothing happened. She gritted her teeth and tried a big tug, and nothing happened. Ingrid set her jaw, braced her feet, and leaned all of her weight backward. With a loud "whoosh," the boot slipped off, Ingrid flopped to the ground, and the boot flew through the air, landing perfectly upright in the chocolate cake.

I braced myself for the anger that was sure to follow.

Nels looked at his wife solemnly, although the ends of his mustache appeared to be quivering. "May I help you up, my dear?" He stood up and offered his hand to his wife. She took the hand and pulled herself up. I couldn't read her expression. Ingrid didn't look at the keeper, which I thought was a bad sign. If I were at home, a yelling match would begin at any moment.

Ingrid brushed her skirts off, smoothed her hair, and then looked at the cake. Then she turned and looked at her husband. *Here it comes,* I thought.

Ingrid started making a funny noise, and the keeper snorted. They were laughing! My mouth hung open. They laughed until everyone joined in except me. When they finally stopped, they collapsed into chairs, the keeper with one boot on and off, Ingrid wiping away tears with her apron.

No one said anything for a moment. Then the keeper winked at me and turned to face his wife. "My dear, would you kindly help me with my other boot?"

"I think not," retorted Ingrid. "You shall have to sleep with one boot on. I have to protect my kitchen. I have already lost a perfectly good chocolate cake."

"I bet it tastes good still," offered James.

"It's got dirt on it!" Nellie scolded.

James grinned. "A little dirt never hurt anything."

"I'll help with the boot, Daddy," said Sarah. James stood up.

"We'll help, too," he said. Nellie and James joined her. They pulled and pulled, the boot came off, and they landed in a dog pile, giggling.

I sat with my mouth hanging open. I had never seen anything like this. No one had yelled; no one had blamed anyone; no one thought that the loss of a chocolate cake was a tragedy or that plopping onto the floor was the end of the world. Maybe these people were crazy.

Everyone sat down again. "Aren't you going to move the boot off the cake, Mother?" asked Nellie.

"No, I think I'll just leave it there. It looks rather good, I think. Nels will have to get another boot."

Nels gnawed on his pipe, James snorted, and Nellie said, "Ick."

We ate the cake after Ingrid scrapped off a layer of frosting. It was to die for.

CHAPTER 8:

Lighthouse Tales

LICKING UP THE CRUMBS FROM my fingers, I debated about asking for another piece.

"Tell us a story, Papa," Sarah begged.

Nels removed his watch from his narrow pocket. "Yes, I have a little time before I must go to the lighthouse. What kind of story?"

"A ghost story," suggested James.

"An exciting rescue," said Sarah.

"A pirate story," said Nellie.

"Tell us a story about all three," I blurted out.

"Hmm. I need a minute to think."

Nels chewed on the end of his pipe. The crackling of wood in the fireplace was the only sound. *If the whole room were looking at me, I would never be able to think of anything.* Nels finally stirred in his rocker. "I'm ready." Everyone drew in closer, and Ingrid picked up some sewing.

"Well, I'm going to tell you about a lighthouse on the ocean. This lighthouse stays open all year, unlike ours, and is surrounded by water. The two keepers became very ill with high fevers and hallucinations. They didn't know where they were or who they were, so they forgot to light the lamps.

"In the middle of the night, the fever of one of the keepers broke and he realized where he was and that he had better get the lamps lit so no ships crashed on the rocks. But when he climbed the stairs to the lighthouse, he found that the lights had already been lit, the wicks trimmed, the lamps filled with kerosene, and the windows scrubbed clean of soot. He knew that there were only two people on the island. So who lit the lights?"

"Ooh," said Sarah.

"One of them probably did it in his sleep," said Nellie.

"That is a creepy story," I said, shivering but delighted. I liked mysteries. "No one ever found out what happened?"

"Never," said Nels. The clock chimed. The keeper rose from his chair. "Time for the lights."

"Oh, Papa, can I come tonight?" begged Sarah, the five-year-old.

"No, sweet pea. You have to be a bit older to work at the lighthouse," said her father. A tear leaked out of her blue eye and splashed on her white nightgown.

"Oh, honey," he picked her up and put her over his shoulder. "Ingrid, Ingrid, I have lost our Sarah and all I can find is this sack of potatoes. What am I to do?" The sack of potatoes giggled and squealed when her father spun around and around. "Ingrid, should I put this sack of potatoes in the cupboard? Or does it go out in the barn?" Everyone laughed except me. Tears stung my eyes. My dad did that once when I was little.

"I think the sack goes in bed," said her mother.

When the keeper came back downstairs, he grabbed his hat. "Paige, would you like to come with me tonight to help? I'm sure Nellie wouldn't mind waiting until tomorrow night for her turn."

"Yes, I'd love ..." I began, but then I looked at Nellie. It was clear that she did mind very much. "Oh well, let Nellie go if it's her turn."

The keeper gave his daughter a "be nice to the company" look. "Nellie, Paige won't be here very long."

I heard Nellie mutter under her breath, "Good!"

The keeper added, "You'll have more opportunities to work in the lighthouse. She won't."

Silence reigned until Nellie said in a rather sulky voice, "Yes, Father. She can have my turn."

"Thank you. You help your mother now. Let's go to work, Paige."

I stole a glance at Nellie's stormy face. I sighed inwardly. *I feel lonely.* I followed the keeper out the door. Maggie stayed at the house.

The keeper's house was about a hundred feet from the base of the lighthouse, where the office sat. We entered the office, and the keeper lit the kerosene lamp on the desk.

"First, we have to fill the upstairs lamps with oil and trim the wicks. Then we light them. We clean the tower windows because the lamps smoke and cloud them up."

We climbed the stairs to the tower. The sun was setting, turning the clouds pink and blue. The sunlight painted a yellow strip on the water, calm for now. The keeper took a moment to gaze at the sunset. "I would do this job for free just for the sunsets," he said. "But don't tell anyone."

When it was time to light the lamps, we got busy. I'd never worked so hard in my life. First, we dug in the oil shed for the kerosene, which was incredibly heavy to carry. The keeper demonstrated how to fill the lamps. Three kerosene lamps burned inside the lens that magnified the light. I learned how to trim the wicks so the flame wouldn't burn too high. If I didn't do it exactly right, he made me do it again, which was not fun. He was very particular.

We cleaned the windows. Then the keeper showed me how to light the lamps and where to put them. We polished the prisms in the lens forever! Soon we spiraled down the steps to the office. He showed me the journal (again) and specified what it was supposed to include: the weather, the direction of the wind, and other information about that day. I noticed he didn't include my visit.

Nels kept up a continuous stream of talk, never seeming to take a breath. He finally paused to drink his coffee, and he offered me some. We sipped the strong brew. It seemed to go with the lighthouse. Though it didn't look dirty to me, we tidied the office in exhaustive detail and scrubbed the circular staircase. I've never cleaned so much in my life. The keeper talked through all of that, too. I didn't mind. No one talks to me at home.

Around midnight, we hiked upstairs to check on the lamps. They needed to be trimmed and filled. And again we had to clean the windows, which were already smeared with soot. The gears needed to be wound again, just like a clock.

"Do you work all night?" I asked.

"Yes, I do."

"When do you sleep?"

"After sunup until about noon. Then I work some more."

I was getting sleepy.

"You look mighty tired. I wanted to ask you more about your time and what it's like, but you better go in to bed. I can always ask you tomorrow." He gave me a kerosene lantern. "Here, it's dark out there. You'll need this."

It was spooky dark. There were no streetlights, only the stars and my lantern, which I held ahead of me so I wouldn't trip. The breeze off the lake felt like cobwebs on my face. I crept up to the spare room.

To my relief, Maggie was there, napping on a white nightgown. I rolled her off and she yawned. I scrambled into the linen gown and dove into bed. Thoughts of a toothbrush flitted in and out of my head. *I'm going to have to figure out what they use.* The bed didn't bounce like mine at home. *I wonder what it's made of,* I thought as I pulled the soft quilt up to my chin. Maggie jumped up on the bed and plopped next to me. I extinguished the lantern.

I thought of my room at home, my hideaway. No one ever came down there, so I was safe from the family fighting, although I could still hear the yelling, the weeping, and the slamming doors.

The quiet whispered with the waves, the wind, and the gulls skirting over the house, crying. Voices murmured. Ingrid sang softly in the next room and a clock ticked. Pleasant, safe sounds filled the house. Even so, tears began to seep into my pillow. *Why am I crying? I can't figure it out.* Maggie stood up on the bed, put her paws on my stomach, and began licking my face. This made me laugh.

"Lie down, you silly dog." I scratched Maggie's ears. She sat down on top of me. "No. Over here." I scooted over, making a space for Maggie. With my hand on her fur and the beam from the lighthouse sweeping over my head, I finally fell asleep.

CHAPTER 9:

I Grow Up and Lose a Hundred Years

I AWOKE TO THE SMELL of frying bacon. I tried to swing my legs over the side of the bed, but I was tangled in the nightgown. I usually wore T-shirts to bed, the older, the better. When I finally got unwound, I stood and peered into the mirror above the dresser. "Ugh," I said. I pushed my bangs away from my face. They shot back. *No comb, no toothbrush, no makeup, no clean clothes.*

Someone knocked. Ingrid bounded in, already looking fabulous, her hair swept up. A few wisps curled down her neck. Her arms were loaded with clothing, and each hand carried a boot.

"Are you awake? I'm so glad. I was worried."

"Why?" I glanced at my wristwatch out of habit, but it hadn't worked since I arrived.

"Yes, my dear, you slept twenty-four hours straight! I kept checking on your breathing, but you seemed to be fine." She dropped the armload of clothes on the bed. "Nels said maybe it had to do with you being from the future."

"I missed a whole day?"

Ingrid nodded and pushed up her spectacles.

"Huh," I mused. "Must be like jet lag or something."

"What's jet lag?" Ingrid asked.

"When you fly somewhere to a different time zone, like Europe, and your body gets tired and out of sync because of the change."

"Fly?"

"In an airplane."

"Really? Like the Wright brothers? Do you fly yourself?"

"No, no." I ran my fingers through my hair. "The pilot flies the plane. I'm just a passenger."

"But have you been to Europe?" asked Ingrid with interest.

"Uh, no."

Ingrid turned back to the bundle on the bed. "I've brought you some clean clothes," she said. "Luckily, you're about my size." She left and returned three more times until a mountain had grown. "I had to look in all the nooks and crannies and trunks, but I found everything you need."

The underwear was bloomers of a soft fabric and a camisole with lace and tiny tuck stitches. Ingrid gave me a skirt and several petticoats to wear underneath. She also brought me a toothbrush at my request. I was glad about that until I learned it was made of boar's bristles.

"These are beautiful," I said about the clothes.

"Thank you. I hand-stitched them myself. All girls are taught to sew. Is that still true in your time?"

I shook my head no.

"I also brought several ridiculous garments. I don't wear these here, but a lady is required to wear them in society. I hope they have better ideas in the future." She showed me a bustle belonging to her mother, a corset, gloves, and a huge hat.

Ingrid demonstrated how the bustle worked. "It makes your backside bigger," she explained.

I thought the bustle was dumb until I tried on the corset.

"This laces tight around your middle and makes your waist tiny."

"But you can't breathe!" I said, taking it off as quickly as possible.

I tried on the gloves and held out my hands. "We don't have to wear hats or gloves. Women still want to have thin waists and have nice behinds ... Oh, sorry. Should I not use that word?"

"Don't worry. Why don't you go behind the screen there and try on the skirt and blouse? If you want to wear the bloomers, I can wash your undergarments."

I went behind the screen. I took off my blue-and-yellow polka-dot bra and the matching panties. I put on the bloomers, which were baggy shorts that descended to my knees, and slipped the camisole and blouse over my head. The skirt cascaded to the floor. I immediately felt older. I swished when I moved. I folded my nightgown neatly and then my bra and panties, and handed the package to Ingrid. She held up the bra.

"My, how colorful! If this is what I have to look forward to, how fun! Would you like me to pin your hair up?"

I nodded. "Now turn around so I can see you," said Ingrid.

I twirled in a circle.

"You look beautiful, dear. I have some combs that would look perfect in your hair. Let me get them." Ingrid returned with a hairbrush, hair pins, and a comb.

She put my hair into some kind of loose bun. I looked in the mirror. It didn't even look like me. Weird.

"You look wonderful. How fun to have another woman here. Come downstairs for breakfast. It's almost ready."

I blushed. At home, no one thought of me as a grown-up.

Ingrid left the room. Then after a few seconds, she popped back in the doorway with her hand on the frame. "Uh, we told the older children about you. I mean about where you came from. They knew it was odd. They know there's no way here except by boat. We didn't tell Sarah."

I followed Ingrid down the stairs. I wasn't used to walking in a long dress. It bunched up between my legs and tripped me. The stairs were steep, so I finally grabbed a handful of fabric and hiked it up to my knees, which got me down the stairs. Sarah caught a glimpse before I dropped my skirts.

"I saw your knees," she announced.

"Sarah, that's not polite," Mom said.

Yesterday you saw a lot more than that.

"You told me not to lift up my skirts," Sarah protested.

"I'm sure that Paige is not used to walking in long skirts," said her mother. She looked at me and smiled. "It takes some getting used to."

I smiled back. I let Maggie outside.

We all sat down to breakfast. James said grace. Eggs and bacon and muffins and milk soon vanished. I stole a glance at Nellie and James. Nellie was definitely still mad at me. James, however, was no longer looking at me with suspicion. He smiled at me once. I was so shocked I forgot to smile back.

"What would you like to do today?" asked Ingrid.

I felt tears gather in my eyes. *Go home.* I opened my mouth but nothing came out. Ingrid noticed my distress.

"You could just stick close by me today. It's washing day for the Christiansens."

The children moaned.

"I also need to bake some bread."

Homesickness was coming over me. Then I felt something tickle my hand. I peeked under the table. It wasn't Maggie. It was a yellow Labrador. Only the tail could be seen wagging above the other end of the table.

"Who let Ralph in?" asked Ingrid. "He's not supposed to be under the table when we're eating." Sarah giggled, but no one owned up.

I patted the soft head. He licked my hand. "How come I haven't met Ralph before?" I asked.

"Ralph likes to go on secret journeys," James said, grinning. "He'll run off for a couple of days and then reappear. Maybe he has a family somewhere in the woods. Or maybe he's catching rabbits. Usually he stinks when he comes back."

Ingrid peered under the table. "Ralph!" she boomed. He turned and pushed past everyone's legs to reach her. "What are you doing under there?" Ralph poked Ingrid with his nose and licked her arm. Her stern face melted into a laugh. "You better not steal any muffins," she said as she scratched his ears.

"Ralph loves muffins," explained James.

Ralph was told to stay. He did. I ate some more muffins because they were so good. I decided I would stick close to Ingrid all day.

"I'll help you with laundry," I offered.

"That would be wonderful," said Ingrid. "Washing clothes in the lake is quite a production. The lighthouse inspector—he makes the rules, you know—said we could have laundry hanging only on Mondays. Isn't that the silliest thing you've ever heard? No road exists to our lighthouse. Who's going to see our clothes flapping in the wind? The gulls on Lake Superior? I'm afraid I don't always follow the rules.

"Nels, dear, why don't you go up to bed?"

Nels hadn't said a word during breakfast. Now his chin bounced on his chest and he was snoring. His head jerked upward at Ingrid's voice. He eased out of the chair, and I soon heard clomping on the stairs.

James grinned at me.

"He's like that every morning. Doesn't hear a thing we say."

I smiled back.

James let Ralph outside. I glanced out and saw Ralph and Maggie chasing each other. We washed the dishes with water from a pump. With everyone helping, it didn't take long.

When the dishes were done, Nellie followed me upstairs and grabbed my arm. "I know you're not from the future." She squeezed my wrist. "Your parents probably dropped you here because they didn't want you. Then you made up that story so my parents would feel sorry for you." She stomped away.

I stood frozen with my mouth hanging open.

No doubt existed about what Nellie thought of me.

Shortly after that, my camera disappeared.

CHAPTER 10:

I Make Plans

After lunch, we washed all of the clothes. This consisted of dunking them in Lake Superior and swishing them with soap. We got soaked. When we got back to the house, we hung up the pants and skirts and socks on the clothes line to flap in the wind like soggy flags.

Nels was awake. He picked up his wife, swung her around, and gave her a kiss on the cheek. Ingrid laughed. *What a good sound.*

We set about making bread. I had never made it before and wanted to learn. Ingrid didn't measure anything. She would say, "Add a pinch of this or a handful of that." Flour covered every surface. Ingredients littered the counters, and lunch dishes soaked in the sink.

"Now the dough must rise," Ingrid explained. "I put it on the back of the stove because it's warm." She tucked a clean, embroidered towel over the top of the crockery bowl and dusted her hands off on her apron.

Ingrid pumped cold water into the sink. Then she poured boiling water into the sink from the iron kettle and handed me a towel.

"I'll wash and you dry," she said, pushing her sleeves above her elbows and sweeping a stray hair behind her ear.

She plunged her hands into the sinkful of dirty dishes and asked me questions about my family.

"So you're the oldest," said Ingrid as she scrubbed a plate. "Tell me about your mother and father."

"My dad is a teacher. He teaches social studies. Civics. Citizenship. You know."

"So who is president in your time?"

"It's a woman. Edith Lewis."

"I'll be. A woman president. I wish I could see that. That's something, all right. I can't even vote."

I had learned that in school, but somehow it had never seemed real. Now the enormous unfairness of denying women the vote struck me.

"Why, that's … terrible." I struggled to remember. "Women get to vote in 1920, I think."

"Really?" said Ingrid. "That's very encouraging. I'll have to remember that when the president annoys me."

I continued, "My mother always voted. She never missed."

"What else? Does your mother manage property?" She hadn't noticed I was using the past tense.

"Sure, she managed our rental properties."

Ingrid looked at me solemnly. "But you're saying *had*. Has your mother passed on?"

Tears came up in my eyes and I nodded. I hate crying.

"I'm so sorry," she said, and was quiet. Then to change the subject, she continued, "My mother wasn't allowed to manage anything. In the law's eyes, all decisions about property were made by my father."

I couldn't believe that this was so. I thought a little more. "My mom owned half of our house. And a car. She had her own bank account. Some of the rental properties were in her name. That's so unfair!"

Ingrid's jaw tightened. "Yes, it is, isn't it?" She was silent for a moment. "But you've given me hope for the future." She turned to face me and smiled. "Time to knead the dough."

I liked kneading. I got to smash and push the dough. It was like playing with sticky clay. We put the dough in long, thin pans to bake. Ingrid brushed butter on the top and then placed them carefully in the cast-iron oven. We went back to washing dishes.

"Tell me about your mother."

"We did dishes together when I was little." I didn't blubber this time. "She died when I was ten."

Ingrid patted my arm. When she did, she got water and soap suds all over me. "Sorry," said Ingrid. "You have some in your hair." She tried to wipe the suds out of my hair but got some on my face.

"Hey, you're getting me all wet. You have some in your hair, too," I said, as I deliberately scooped up a handful of water and soapsuds and deposited them on Ingrid's head. I was scared for a minute because at home this would cause a war. But Ingrid got the giggles. Soon I was laughing, too.

"It's a new hairdo," said Ingrid, patting her head. "I think this style would look lovely on you." We started laughing so hard we were crying and had to sit down.

"What's going on?" James burst through the door. I opened my mouth to tell him but was seized by another fit of giggles. "Really, Mother," he said. "It's not very dignified." For some reason, this made Ingrid laugh even harder. We had to dry our eyes with our aprons, only I forgot and used my skirt, and then we wiped our heads with a towel.

"Well, that certainly felt good," said Ingrid. She dabbed her arm again. "But we better check the bread so it doesn't burn." Ingrid opened the oven, and the most delicious smell wafted through the kitchen.

"That smells incredible," I said. Two more heads popped through the door.

"The bread smells so good," said Nellie.

"Can we have some?" asked Sarah.

"Of course, when it's finished."

"My ma makes the best bread and butter in the whole world," bragged Nellie.

I looked up with interest. "You make your own butter?"

"Yes," said Sarah. "We have a cow. Her name is Daisy. James milks her twice a day."

"We have a horse, too," said Nellie, interrupting her.

"I'd like to learn how to make butter," I said. "Could I ride your horse, too?"

"Do you know how?" asked James.

"Actually, I do. I do English horse riding."

"Oh, that's sissy stuff. I mean like cowboy riding."

"There are no cowboys left," I said.

"Oh, yeah? What do you know?"

"I know a hundred years' more history than you," I blurted out.

"Well, you'll just have to show me that you can ride," James blustered.

"Okay, I will."

"And I can teach you how to milk," he offered, needing the last word and getting it.

"I'll teach you the butter," offered Sarah. "Ma lets me churn. That's how you do it."

I looked over at Nellie. She glared at me, making it plain she wouldn't be helping. *Oh, let her rot. Her attitude is ticking me off. What have I ever done to her?*

Ingrid checked the bread again. She pulled the hot pan from the oven with a towel.

As soon as we could touch the bread without burning our fingers, we tore off chunks and dipped them in the butter.

"This is the best bread I have ever tasted," I said. "The kind my stepmom buys tastes like plastic."

All of the blond heads at the table looked at me.

"What's plastic?" asked James.

"I dunno. It's hard. They make stuff out of it. It's like ... indestructible," I explained.

"Indestructible bread. That doesn't sound very good," said Ingrid.

"That's sad, Paige," said Sarah, with her mouth full. I had to agree with her.

That night, I went to bed early. I was tired. I turned down an invitation to the lighthouse. Nellie went instead. I had managed to sneak out to the lighthouse with Maggie earlier in the day to touch the journal, but nothing happened.

Once I got to my bedroom, my loneliness hit me like a storm. I cried. Maggie looked at me. Then she decided to sit on me. She weighs seventy pounds and thinks I'm her personal mattress, pillow, servant, slave, butler, or whatever she wants at that moment.

"No. Here." I scooted over, making a space. She took up half of the bed and she snored big time, but I didn't mind. With my hand on Maggie's fur, I finally fell into the sweet oblivion of sleep.

CHAPTER 11:

Morning Chores

THE NEXT DAY AFTER BREAKFAST, James offered to take me to the barn.

"You're not mad at me?" I asked.

"Who, me?" he said. "Why should I be mad?"

"Nellie is."

"Oh, well, it takes her awhile to warm up to new folk."

That's the understatement of the year. We walked to the chicken coop, and James showed me how to scatter feed on the ground for the chickens. He took down a wire basket from a nail. While the chickens ate, he went to the coop and began collecting eggs. I picked up one.

"Why is it warm?" I asked, cupping it gently in my hand.

"It was just laid," said James.

We gathered all the eggs. I liked to follow the chickens around and watch them strut and scratch the ground. "They're funny," I said. "Their heads bobble up and down," and I demonstrated, laughing.

James paused in his work to watch. He scratched his head, puzzled. He never did see the humor in it.

"Here, why don't you take these eggs up to Ma? I gotta milk the cow."

I delivered the basket to the kitchen table and returned to the barn. I sank down on a bale of hay.

I love barns, especially my horse's barn. I like the smell of hay and leather saddles, the scent of horses, even when they're sweaty. At home, if I came at feeding time, the horses would nicker softly with excitement. When I visited the stalls, Cyrus would blow on my face and Gus would bob his head up and down for a carrot. If visitors sat on the bench below Gus's window, he would nibble their hair. Picasso would be soaking his tail in the water bucket and then would flip around to stick his long, fuzzy nose through the feeding slot, hoping for a nice scratch. My eyes filled with tears. This crying thing was getting to be a bad habit. I shook my head hard and tried to focus on now.

Maggie was sticking her nose into various containers to see what the smells were all about. At the hay bale, she sneezed.

James was sitting on a short wooden stool, talking to the cow. "Hey, you old Daisy," he said. She mooed. He scratched her ears. He milked for a while. The milk squirted into a metal bucket, making a tapping-tin noise. Then I heard a whinny. My head popped up and I looked around.

"The horse is in here? I thought he was in the other barn."

"Naw. He likes being with Daisy. If he's not with Daisy, he whinnies real loud. Makes my ears hurt."

I wrapped my shawl around me and walked over to the stall to see a horse looking at me. I had time only to register that it was a big horse, more than sixteen hands, before James called me back.

"Milk's done. Come have a drink."

Steam rose from the bucket. James took a tin cup off of a nail and dipped it into the bucket. He took a long drink. A white line dribbled down his chin. He wiped it off with his shirt sleeve and grinned. "It's good."

James scooped a tinful and handed it to me. I took a sip—warm and delicious!

"Our milk is always cold," I said. "But it never tastes this good."

"Fresh from the cow," said James. "I'm going to have a farm and sell milk when I grow up."

"You don't want to be a lighthouse keeper?"

"If what you say is true, there won't be lighthouse keepers for long."

"But that doesn't happen for fifty or sixty years."

He was silent while he did the math. "I'll be as old as sin. Will you be alive then?"

"No, I won't be born yet."

"We won't know each other then," said James.

"I guess not."

"Well, as long as you're here, be useful and take the milk up to Ma."

I grinned. So much for sentiment. Somehow I knew James was glad I was here, even though he would never say so in a million years.

As I trudged to the house, the milk slapping against the sides of the bucket, I tried to remember "my time." It was becoming a little foggy.

When I returned from the house, James was pitching hay for Daisy and the horse. I wandered over to the horse's stall. The horse looked at me expectantly, not afraid, but just waiting.

"What's the horse's name?"

"Gulliver," said James in a muffled voice.

"Hi, Gulliver." I turned to James. "Do you keep any horse treats?"

James reached into the pocket of his overalls, plucked out a carrot, and handed it to me. "Fresh from the garden," he said. "Gulliver loves them."

I walked back to the stall. The horse's ears were pricked, alert. Mice darted in and out. I grabbed my skirt, pulled it up, and tucked it into my waist. It was probably illegal or something, but at least mice wouldn't run under my dress.

This thought made me shudder. I turned my attention back to the horse.

His nose was quivering, which meant that he could smell the carrot. I held it out as a peace offering. The horse considered it, decided it was safe, and meandered over to me, neck outstretched. I gave him the carrot, and he crunched on it. When he was finished, bits of carrot drooled down his jaw.

"My, you're a messy eater." The horse tossed his head sideways, his mane lifting. I approached him quietly, wanting to pat his neck. He shied away a bit but then stood still. I rubbed his neck.

"Hey, boy, what a beautiful horse you are. You're very big!" The horse stamped his front hoof. "You think so, too, eh? What kind of horse is he?" I asked James, who was fixing Daisy's stall door.

"He's just a plain brown horse."

"Don't listen to him," I said to the horse. "You are very beautiful." Gulliver nickered.

I poked around for a grooming brush. I found one and started brushing the horse's soft coat. I rubbed his nose, which was like velvet. Gulliver snuffled around the pockets of my apron.

"Looking for more carrots? I'm sorry. I don't have any more." I scratched his ears to see if he was the type of horse that liked ear-rubbing. If you touched the ears of Punkin, a horse at home, she would try to kick you. I sighed. I missed Punkin. That old horse, saved from the glue factory, with all her stubborn ways, had taught me to ride.

I found a pitchfork and began mechanically to pick up the manure. I did it at home and it was automatic. I didn't mind. It didn't smell that bad and it made the horses happy because there were fewer flies.

I had a pitchforkful and then realized that I didn't know where to put it. "James, where do you put the manure?"

He looked at me in surprise. "What are you doing that for?"

I looked at him in surprise. "Don't you do it every day?"

"I never seen a girl groom b'fore."

Normally, this would have offended me, but I was starting to get used to the hundred-year time change.

"Well, if you don't want me to help, I don't have to," I began, knowing that everyone wants help cleaning up horse poop.

"Oh, sure, you can help," James said quickly. "Take it out back. There's a pile. We use the muck in the garden."

"Do you have a muck bucket?" He showed me where it was and then continued to clean the cow's stall. I dumped the manure in the bucket. We both cleaned quietly.

"Don't you have a radio?"

"Naw. I read about them and how they work. Sound and music get transmitted through a box."

"Yeh."

"Nah, we don't have one. But I want to get one."

"It plays music. It helps pass the time, and the horses like it. But I forgot, you need electricity. Or batteries."

James stopped and leaned on the pitchfork to listen. "I've heard of that. I like to read about science and stuff. Is the future great?"

I had never really thought about it before. "Well, you can stay up later because the house has light. And the whole house is always warm in the winter and cool in the summer. The stove you just turn on, no wood or fire. It's a lot easier. You just flick a button." I thought of all the other things (like the shower) that I missed. Then I thought of my family. "It's all right, I guess … I hope someone is taking care of my horse."

James looked interested. "Tell me about your horse."

I smiled. "Her name is Wildheart."

"Is she fast?"

"Oh, yeah."

He grinned. "Gulliver here is mighty fast. Betcha can't ride him."

CHAPTER 12:

I Ride a Horse, of Course

Annoyance prickled the back of my neck and I could feel red creep into my face. I won ribbons at shows for my riding abilities.

"Betcha I can."

"Let's see."

We walked to the other side of the barn. On the wall, horse tack, hoof picks, brushes, combs, and an assortment of horse-related items hung from hooks and nails that pegged the wood. On the floor stood two roughhewn sawhorses carrying saddles waiting for riders. The saddle leather was worn but a rich color, and the scent of saddle oil lingered in the air.

"This one's yours." James pointed to one. I lifted it off of the sawhorse. Then I put it back. It had two horns instead of one.

"What kind of saddle is this?"

"A side saddle. It's for girls."

Vague images of my great-grandmother's side saddle abandoned in the garage floated up in my memory, but I didn't know how to ride on one. It looked like you'd kill yourself.

"Why does it have two horns?"

"It's so you can ride wearing a dress. My mother rides this way. It's called riding 'aside.' Your left foot goes in the stirrup and your right leg goes over this horn above your other leg."

I was incredulous. "You've got to be kidding. You mean both legs are on the left side? How in heaven's name am I supposed to balance?"

"Beats me. Seems mighty awkward. I never figured out how Ma could do it."

"Well, I can't use that thing. I'll fall right off. I'll use the other saddle." I lifted it off of the sawhorse.

"You're going to ride astride?"

"I don't know what you're talking about. I'm going to put a foot in each stirrup and ride."

James looked scandalized. "Girls don't do that, you know. Not without a split skirt."

"Girls from your time, you mean." I lifted the other saddle and the blanket and began to put it on Gulliver. He was a tall horse, sixteen and four hands, so I dragged the milking stool over to stand on. James watched for a minute and then began to help me. We got the saddle on.

"Could you bridle him, since I'm not used to him?" I asked.

"Sure. He's pretty good about it. I got bit just once, and that was my fault for sticking my finger too far in his mouth."

After bridling the horse, James led him out of the stall and onto the grass. Gulliver started munching.

"Could you hold him please?" I asked. "My horse likes to walk off when I'm half on."

James grabbed the reins and watched. I lifted up my left foot to put it in the stirrup, but the skirt tripped me halfway. I tried again, but the skirt's A-line cut wasn't full enough to allow me to lift my foot into the stirrup. I pulled my skirt up above my knees and tried again.

I got my left foot into the stirrup. Then I leaned forward and started to swing my right leg over the horse. The skirt halted me in mid-motion and I almost fell backward off the horse.

I pulled the skirt higher, swung my leg over, and heard a big rip. Now I was in the saddle but the skirt was all bunched up around my legs. I tried to arrange it so at least I could get my feet in the stirrups. I ended up grabbing my skirt and hiking it up to my thighs.

I looked over at James, who was staring at me.

"What are you looking at?" I grumbled as I tried to get comfortable.

James flushed. "Not supposed to see a girl's legs."

"You can't see my legs. All you can see is my tights."

"Still, they're nice legs."

I blushed. "If you came to my time, you'd be able to see a lot more than just legs."

"Really? That'd be something." He grinned again. "Like what?"

I grinned back. "Never mind. I'm going to ride now."

"You sure you're all organized?" I nodded. "Now let's see you ride that horse."

I took the reins and gave the horse a tiny kick. Gulliver began walking really fast. He had a bumpy gait, and I went up and down as he walked in a circle.

"He likes to jump," said James.

"Ho," said I, telling Gulliver to stop. "Really? What do you jump?"

"Low fences, bushes. We made a short fence over there." He pointed to the other side of the yard.

I gave Gulliver a bigger kick and he began to trot, one, two, three, four. It felt good. It seemed like forever since I had ridden. I laughed. "It's been a hundred years since I've ridden." The laugh made me loosen the hold on the reins a little and Gulliver went faster and began to canter. I counted in my head: one, two, three. His canter was smoother, and I had no trouble staying in sync with the motion.

I did a circle and came back to James. "Ho!" The horse stopped on a dime, throwing me forward onto his neck. "Wow!"

"Yeh, he's good. I taught him to stop fast."

A sudden desire to ride as fast as I could overtook me. I knew this was a stupid idea. I could hear my teacher telling me to take it slow with an unknown horse. "You don't know them and you don't know what they'll do." I completely ignored this wise advice. I turned the horse around and told him to trot. He trotted immediately. I told him to go faster.

"Hey, what do you think you're doing?" I heard James yell. I kept going. Soon the horse was at a gallop. I forgot about being stuck in the past, about the parts of home that I missed. I just enjoyed the ride, the sound of the hooves, the air rushing by my ears.

As bumpy as he was and as fast as we were going, I didn't have any trouble staying on. I had a good seat, my teacher had said. We rode to the edge of the clearing.

I told Gulliver to turn, but he didn't, and I had the first inkling that I might have lost control of the horse. I was headed straight for a tree. I pulled the reins right. He didn't turn right. He kept going. Serious fear enveloped me. "Ho! Ho!" I yelled, pulling harder on the reins. He ignored me.

Just when I was sure we were going to run headlong into the tree, he veered right, without slowing down. I lost my balance and one of the stirrups but didn't fall off. I was tempted to close my eyes. Gulliver continued to run. He headed for a bush. I again tried to get him to turn. I realized he was going to jump it. I held on, leaned forward, and lifted my rear end out of the saddle. He sailed through the air and over the bush without much effort. I landed with a bump in the saddle, and both my feet came out of the stirrups. I still had the reins. *A lot of good that is doing.* The horse continued to jump: over a stack of wood, a bale of hay, and an overturned rowboat. Each time I closed my eyes, but I made it.

Gulliver was coming upon the barn again, and James was waving his hands. The horse continued to run right up to James and then just halted. Not ready for the sudden stop, I kept going and did a somersault over the horse's neck, landing on my tailbone on the ground.

"Ouch," was my comment after several seconds of stunned silence.

James ran over to me. "Are you all right?" Gulliver stood nearby chomping on grass, unconcerned or possibly pleased at the havoc he had caused...

I looked up into the sky without moving. James reached out a hand to help me up.

"I think I need a minute." James sat down beside me on the ground, cross-legged. I lifted my arms from behind me, where they had landed, and moved them tentatively. My wrist hurt like heck where I braced myself on the ground, but it still moved and I didn't think it was broken. My arms were covered with dirt. I started brushing them off.

I moved my legs. They still worked, too. It was a miracle. I thought I'd better pull my skirt down over my knees, so I did.

"You have grass in your hair," James said.

I said, "Oh, well." I lay back down on the ground. "I think I'll just stay here." I hoped I would be able to get up. As I lay there, Gulliver meandered over and blew on my face. I had to laugh. "Well, Gulliver, I guess you showed me."

"I guess he did," said James. "But you took them jumps pretty well."

"I had my eyes closed," I said. The absurdity of it all struck me. I started laughing. James started laughing, too. "I must have come here to learn horse jumping."

"You must have come here to learn how to fall off a horse."

I tried to brush off the dirt.

"I'm thinking Ma will insist on a bath," said James, looking at me.

"Really?" I said. I hadn't had a bath since I'd arrived. We seemed to do a lot of washing up from a basin and pitcher or rinsing off in the cold lake, but there was no tub or shower. "How?"

"The tub gets put in the kitchen and then you heat up the water on the stove and keep pouring it in. The kitchen is off limits when someone is taking a bath."

The idea of sitting naked in a tiny metal tub in the middle of the kitchen was not reassuring.

CHAPTER 13:

A Newfangled Tub

I LIMPED INTO THE KITCHEN. James followed me. Ingrid turned around. "Hello, I ... What in heaven's name happened to you?"

Everyone in the kitchen was looking at me. My cheeks got hot and I wanted to hide. I started to say I fell off the horse but James jumped in.

"Gulliver took off with her and threw her." I looked at James and his mouth was twitching.

Ingrid put her hands, which were all floury, on her hips. "That horse. He has a few nasty tricks." She peered closely at me and reached out to wipe some dirt from my cheek. "Looks like you need to take a bath."

"But Mama, it's not Sunday tomorrow," said Sarah.

"Well, this is a special occasion."

"Do I look that bad?"

"Go take a look. And James, will you please get the tub?"

I went to find the beveled mirror in the living room. My hair had completely fallen down, and I had hay sticking in it. My face and neck were smeared with dirt. That was all I could see in the tiny mirror. "Drat that horse," I said, and then smiled.

I returned to the kitchen. Big cast-iron pots littered the stovetop. A tin tub, like I used for bobbing for apples, squatted in the middle of the floor. I wouldn't call it a bathtub. From somewhere, a couple of makeshift curtains had been erected around the tub. Everyone except for Ingrid had disappeared from the kitchen.

"Hi, honey. Why don't you go get some clean clothes from my room while I heat up this water and then you can have a nice bath?"

I trudged up the stairs, my backside groaning in protest. "Ouch." I grabbed some clothes, wishing I could just put on shorts and a T-shirt, but instead grabbed bloomers, a camisole, a blouse, a petticoat, a skirt, and some stockings.

When I got back downstairs, Ingrid poured steaming water into the tub. "How can I take a bath in boiling water?" I asked.

"Oh, I added some cold water from the pump. See how the water feels to you."

I stuck my hand in the water. "Good."

"Well, then, I will leave you be. Here's some soap. Hand me your skirt so I can mend it." Ingrid pulled the curtains tightly around the tub and I was surrounded. I got undressed and tossed the dirty skirt over the curtains to her. "Thanks, Ingrid!"

"You're welcome, my dear. Just have a nice hot soak."

Even though there were curtains, taking a bath in the middle of the kitchen wasn't too private. I stood there looking at the tub. It was small.

I stepped into the tub with both feet and then stepped back out. *How am I supposed to fit?* I tried lowering my behind into the water with my legs hanging over the side. This was very uncomfortable. I pulled my feet inside the tub and sat cross-legged. This was better but not great. I tried bringing my knees up to my chin and then just sat there. The water felt nice. *I haven't had a bath for about a hundred years.* This joke made me feel better.

Soon the water was getting dirty and my skin was feeling nice and clean. Since I couldn't move around, I couldn't figure out how to wash my hair, but I washed my face and neck. Ingrid had left me a towel. I could have soaked longer but Ingrid had food in the oven. I grabbed the towel, dried off quickly, and got dressed as fast as I could. I didn't have a brush, but I finger-combed the hay out of my hair and then swept it up.

I heard a little voice say, "Are you done? I'm very hungry."

I smiled. "Yes, Sarah, I'm done." *With the smallest bath in the world.*

CHAPTER 14:

Can I Tell the Future?

THAT EVENING, I FELT REFRESHED from my bath. My backside still ached. The family voted to play charades. I hesitated to join. At home, when we acted out phrases for people to guess, we always used movie stars and rock groups. For the Christiansens, none of those things existed.

Their charades consisted of books from before 1910. I knew a few of those from English Lit. And they acted out historical figures like Abraham Lincoln and George Washington. I guessed a few.

The family also played a game where each person attempted to name the states in alphabetical order. I messed up with Alaska, which didn't become a state until 1959. When I said, "Alaska," Ingrid and Nels both looked at me with interest. "You mean we're not done with forty-six states?" asked Nels.

"Uh, no, New Mexico, Arizona, Alaska, and Hawaii become states yet." In third grade, I learned a song of all the states.

Nels suggested the kids get some cookies and milk. Sarah scurried away willingly, but James and Nellie protested. Nels's face tightened and his mouth thinned.

"Go," he said. "We need to talk privately." He pointed to the kitchen.

They stomped off.

Ingrid stayed.

Nels rubbed his mustache. I braced myself.

"I'd like to ask some questions. I don't know if you'll want to answer."

I didn't know either, but I nodded.

"To some extent, you know the future," began Nels.

My stomach did a flip-flop.

Ingrid put a hand on Nels's arm. "Nels, do we really want to know the future? Won't it add a huge burden to life? We won't be able to change anything. Won't we worry more about the children and what will happen to them?"

Nels took his wife's hand and kissed it.

"Ingrid, forewarned is forearmed. I really want to know. Perhaps you'd like to skip this conversation?"

"Yes. I'll get the children ready for bed." She stopped in the doorway with her hand on the frame, but didn't turn to face us. "Nels Lars Christiansen, you're being very foolish." Each word cut the air.

Nels rubbed his mustache. He waited until the sound of his wife's footsteps faded. "Is there a war coming up? I've heard rumblings in Europe."

I thought back to American history. This was 1910. I had to memorize the wars in school. World War I was 1914 to 1918, then World War II … .and a whole bunch more. I felt cold and clammy and didn't feel like talking.

"World War I begins in 1914," I answered slowly.

"They start numbering the wars?" Nels gnawed on his pipe.

"Yeah," I said, looking down at my hands.

"That is a bad thing," Nels said. "How many more wars?"

I didn't answer.

He turned away and stared into the flames of the fire. His face turned gray. "I don't suppose you know if I enlist and get killed?"

I shook my head. I was glad I didn't know. I didn't mention that I could look it up at home on the Internet. We sat in silence for a long time.

Nels sighed. "My wife is usually right about these things. She's smart that way." He thought for a moment. "Is the US taken over by another country in these wars?"

"No," I said.

"Can men travel to the stars in the future?"

"Yes. It's very exciting!"

I told him of the missions to the moon and to Mars.

"Well, I'll be. I'd love to see that. Sailors for centuries have used the stars to navigate." Nels stroked his beard. "Have you traveled to the moon?"

I laughed. "No, just specially trained astronauts. Maybe someday regular people will go."

Still chewing on his pipe, Nels grew quiet. How was there any pipe left? His rocking chair squeaked. I began to think of other events besides wars, like the Great Depression in the 1930s. I hoped Nels was done asking about the future.

He stretched. "I don't want to know more. Now I can dream of jumping to the moon."

He laid his pipe on the table. "You won't mention any of this to my wife, will you?"

I shook my head no. I was done talking.

"Time for me to head to the lighthouse. Goodnight." His back hunched as he walked out of the room.

I trudged upstairs. Knowing the future wasn't as great as I'd always thought it would be.

When I got to my room, I found my camera resting on the dresser, bashed and battered, the memory chip missing. All of my photos of the lighthouse were gone, along with my hopes of posting my lighthouse photos on the Internet site.

I punched my pillow so many times feathers floated in the air. Maggie got scared, and I had to coax her out of the corner. Then I remembered. I didn't know if I was going home. I punched my pillow more. A single feather hung in the air, like my future.

CHAPTER 15:

A Routine of Days

As MY DAYS SPUN INTO a pattern, I felt less lonely. Thoughts of Gran and the good parts of home always hovered close, but I liked the Christiansens, the lighthouse, and the chores. James and I fed the animals every morning and cleaned the barn. James taught me to milk the cow. (Can you believe that?) We drank fresh milk. Later, we helped Ingrid separate the cream and the milk and churned the cream into butter.

After milking, we'd go up to breakfast. Ingrid made the most incredible breakfasts of pancakes, eggs, homemade bread, and bacon. I wondered if I could go back to cold cereal.

Nels would go to bed after breakfast. When he nodded off at the table, he awoke with a snort, much to his children's delight (and mine). During the day, all of us helped Ingrid with the house chores. We usually got part of the afternoon off. James and I rode the horse, fished off the dock, or played chess. Sometimes I would win; sometimes James would win. We also went swimming in the lake. To keep warm, we raced. I always won. For a boy, James took it pretty well. At my real mom's insistence, I had taken many swimming lessons, eventually earning my lifesaving award.

Nellie never joined us, even though I heard she used to do these activities with James. She often watched us from a distance. I wasn't big on Nellie. I admit I stooped so low as to put a dead fish in her bed. She never said anything, but several days later, Maggie and I found a dead mouse in our bed. Maggie found it first, scooped it up, and ran around with the tail sticking out of her mouth, thinking it was a great toy. I dragged her to the barn where she deposited the mouse upon the manure pile. After this, I asked James about Nellie.

James snorted. "She's just jealous. You should have seen her when Sarah was born. She cried and cried and said Ma didn't love her anymore. Sheesh. Half the time, she can't even remember why she's mad. She always has her feathers in a flurry about something."

After supper, we gathered in the parlor to play games or listen to Nels tell stories. At 8 p.m., he would leave for the lighthouse. Nellie, James, and I took turns going with him. I went whenever I could. I loved the lighthouse. I loved being close to the stars and higher than anyone for miles. I liked watching for lights from ships, knowing we were saving them from crashing into the rocks. And I never tired of the view of the lake or the sunsets.

Sometime each day, I snuck out to the lighthouse alone and touched the journal. Nothing ever happened. I did it automatically, not expecting it to take me home. But still I touched it every day.

At midnight, I'd fall into bed exhausted and get up at six to start the whole routine over again. I liked it though. Before I knew it, I'd been there for a whole month.

Then I had a visitor.

CHAPTER 16:

Something Extraordinary Happens

After breakfast one day, I was alone in Ingrid's parlor. I knew I should get up to help in the kitchen, but I felt so tired. I had put my booted feet up on the étagère, and my long skirts tumbled to the floor. A loud thud came from the china cabinet. I sat up, startled.

I jumped up off the fainting couch. I heard a voice.

"Halooo! Boo ho! Open the door!"

I walked slowly to the cabinet and pulled the door open. I stepped back. A long, skinny leg with a huge army boot on it emerged. Next a long arm shot out, with a tattered jacket that stopped at the elbow. Then a head ducked out, topped by a stovepipe hat that was tipped askew. The rest of the body unfolded and stood before me. The person took off his top hat. He dusted off the hat and straightened his red tie. His head hovered close to the ceiling, and his shoulders were stooped, as if he were continually bending over and getting stuck. He bowed.

I stared. "Who are you?" I stammered.

"Mr. Thompson, time traveler."

I continued to stare at him.

"Time traveler. Like you. Jump from century to century."

I was having trouble understanding his odd way of talking, but I figured out what he was saying. "I thought ending up in 1910 was a bad accident," I said.

Mr. Thompson sat down on the couch. He looked like an adult in a child's chair, with his knees poking up next to his neck.

"No, no. No fluke, no aberration, no goof. You're a time traveler. Always have been, always will be." He grabbed his lapels and hung on to them for emphasis.

I didn't doubt that he was a time traveler. After all, he arrived in a china cabinet. But I was annoyed. I put my hands on my hips. "Well, nice of you to finally show up. Why didn't you come sooner? I've been freaking out. Who decided I would come here? You?"

"Me? No ho, no ho. If I were deciding, I'd always go somewhere warm instead of flitting somewhere cold, with snow and glaciers and freezing rain. We're here in Minnesota, and this is summer? What is it? About fifty-five degrees? And these buzzing things flying around? Not summer. Summer is sand and hot sun."

Mr. Thompson pulled a red handkerchief the size of a pillowcase from his pocket. He blew his nose, sounding like a horse snorting.

"That handkerchief is the size of a boat sail," I complained. I didn't know why I was so crabby. "Do you have the power to send me back?" I think that was it. That was what was making me so mad.

Just then we heard voices in the corridor.

"Ho, find another place to talk."

He grabbed my hand. Before I could whisk it back, a large hole had opened up in the floor and Mr. Thompson had stepped into it, dragging me with him. A long sensation of falling raised butterflies in my stomach.

We landed on our feet with a soft thud, as if we had jumped off of a swing. A dome resembling an umbrella appeared over our heads. The clear dome continued to descend, closing under our feet with a loud click, like a door shutting.

Mr. Thompson pointed to the curved walls. "Time bubble," he said.

I remained hunched over, glancing at the ceiling every few seconds. I looked down. Water lapped at my feet, like in a boat. "What is a time bubble?" I asked.

"Float here on Lake Superior. Invisible."

It did feel oddly like a boat bobbing up and down. The bubble was clear, and I could see the gray water beneath my feet. I looked up. I could also see the lake and the sun glinting off the water. There was no place to sit down.

"What year is this please?" I asked.

"Outside of time."

"Why are we here?"

"Need to talk."

"Who are you again?"

"Mr. Thompson, time traveler. You are one, too."

"How could that be?"

"Well, evidence?" He bent down and rolled up his trouser leg, revealing very skinny ankles, with socks and sock girdles, the elastic straps that hold up socks. "Wet feet, bah," he said. He stood back up. "The evidence you're in 1910. You're floating on the lake, invisible. Unusual, don't you think?" He smiled at me.

I looked down at my floor-length frock and my lace-up boots. I had to concede that I was in 1910 clothes. "I thought maybe I was having a really long dream."

"No, really 1910. You're a time traveler, and I'm here to talk."

"About what?"

"Your gift."

"I don't have any gifts. That's what my family says."

"Fools!" I looked at his face, which had turned red, but he didn't seem to be angry with me. "Lies. Evil."

"You." He pointed at me. "Extraordinary gifts." He was silent for a moment. "You were chosen with care. Intelligent, caring, curious, kind, adjustable." He smiled again. "And my favorite, a smartie pants."

"Smartie pants? I haven't heard that term for a century at least."

"See?"

I smiled. "I've missed my dad and gran terribly." This last part I whispered.

"Yes. But your job."

"What is my job?" I was getting used to his odd sentences.

"Help people in dire circumstances."

I looked at him. "Are you an angel?"

"No. That would be an honor. I'm a servant."

The impact of the words "dire circumstances" finally sunk in. "Are the Christiansens in trouble?"

"Not yet, but soon. Need you."

"Are Gran and Dad all right? Do they know I'm gone?"

"No. Fine."

"What am I supposed to do?"

He was silent for a moment. "Don't know."

"You don't *know*?" I admit it. I yelled. I couldn't believe it! What was the point of time travel if you didn't know what was going to happen? "Can't you just pop ahead in time and see?" I asked at my sarcastic best.

"Against rules. Enemies would notice. You're on your own."

I was scared, and it made me mad. "I can't believe you run around sending people on dangerous missions, and you don't know what's going to happen. It's the stupidest thing I've ever heard! What if something happens to me?"

"Risk, indeed."

"So," I said, my sarcasm running high again, "you want me to do something, but I don't know what and I could get hurt in the process. Why should I do that?"

"Helping Christiansens. Helping yourself."

"Well, the whole thing seems very inefficient. Who's in charge?"

"Meet Master later. His rules."

"Bother his rules." I stomped my foot, and water splashed my dress and Mr. Thompson's rolled-up pants.

Mr. Thompson's voice was gentle. "Carefully chosen. Many gifts."

I had never heard this before. I knew I had many faults, like my explosions of anger. Did I really have many gifts?

"Help the Christiansens?"

It was a challenge. I loved a challenge. I had never been known to turn one down. Nobody ever needed me before. I realized I cared about the keeper's family, even Nellie.

I thought a minute. "Yes, whatever."

Mr. Thompson smiled. "Excellent. Look for opportunities to help."

"I still don't get it," I said.

"You will," said Mr. Thompson.

The next thing I knew I was standing ankle-deep in Lake Superior, boots wet and the hem of my dress getting progressively wetter.

I hurried to the house, sure I had been gone for hours. But I glanced at the clock, and I hadn't missed any time at all. I ran upstairs to change before anyone noticed I was dripping wet.

CHAPTER 17:

Our Boat Comes In

THE NEXT MORNING, SARAH BURST into the kitchen. "The boat's here." Then she ran out the back door, slamming it.

"Oh, my," said Ingrid. "I hope I look presentable for guests. We never have company, you know, unless they arrive by boat." I refrained from pointing out that I was a guest and I had not arrived by boat. Ingrid brushed stray hair out of her eyes and walked to the looking glass to inspect her face.

I washed my hands at the pump. "What boat?" I asked, drying my hands on a towel fashioned from a flour sack.

"The supply boat," said Ingrid, as she straightened her spectacles. "It brings us what we need for the lighthouse and for cooking. Let's go, shall we?" Ingrid led the way out of the back door. She picked up her skirts and started running.

I was astonished.

"I hope they brought what I ordered," Ingrid hollered at me.

I took off, too, and found that running in skirts was complicated. I had to hold the layers taut so they didn't bunch up between my legs and trip me. James and Nellie were ahead on the path to the lake, and I could hear Nels coming up behind me.

"I can't wait to see what they brought," yelled Nellie.

The whole family congregated on the dock. A rowboat headed toward us, and out on the water was a much bigger boat. Sarah patted my hand. "It's the lighthouse boat," she explained. "It brings us good things."

We watched as the rowboat inched toward us. As it got closer, I could see two men and some wooden crates.

I began to feel excited, too. The boat finally arrived at the dock. James and Nels tied her up and the two sailors hopped out. "Hello, Sven. Hello, Joe," called Nels, shaking hands. Joe was tall and his shirt billowed in the wind around his skinny body. Sven had a scraggly gray beard and a red face.

"Hello, Mrs. Christiansen. You are looking more beautiful than ever," said Sven. Ingrid laughed. He shook James and Nellie's hands. "Hello, Miss Sarah. You're growing up fast." He grasped her small hand.

"I'm five," she announced.

"I know. I brought you a present." He reached in his coat pocket and pulled out a handful of yellow fluff.

Sarah squealed. "A baby chick! Can I hold him?"

"Of course. He's yours. Hold your hands like a cup." Sven showed her how and then deposited the chick in her hands.

"He's soft," she said. "I'm going to call him Sven."

Sven chuckled. "I've never had a chicken named after me. Thank you very much."

"What do you say, Sarah?" Ingrid prompted.

"Thank you, Sven." She turned around and started hiking to the house, cradling her baby.

Sven worked his way down the row of people. I was last. "And who might you be?"

"Paige. Paige Johnson. I'm a, er, visiting."

"Pleased to meet you."

I discovered a lot of work had to be done before any other surprises. The smaller boat made a number of trips to the bigger boat to refill with supplies. We unloaded kerosene, millions of gallons, it seemed to me. There were also wicks, huge bags of flour and sugar, cans of paint, a hammer and nails, and a cast-iron pot.

"Oh, good," said Ingrid. "Now I can cook up some soup." She grabbed the pot by the handle, and everyone else picked up a burden and headed up the hill. The men carried the kerosene, which was the heaviest. I carried a can of paint in each hand.

This continued for a while until everything was transported to the house. Then the atmosphere changed. Everyone got excited again and ran back to the dock.

Sven handed out more presents, which Ingrid had ordered. Nels got another pipe. Ingrid got a bolt of cotton fabric. For Nellie, Sven pulled out a small wooden chest. "Lighthouse lending library #7" was stamped on the side.

"Ooh!" Nellie exclaimed. "More books! Thank you." She opened the box, and Nellie, James, and I looked inside.

A whole slew of books. I had already read every book at the lighthouse, including one on sewing for amateurs and a chemistry textbook. *More books!* I sighed with happiness.

Next, Sven brought out a box. It had a children's drawing on it. "For James," he said.

"What is it?" asked James.

"See for yourself."

James opened the box. There was another square box inside, which I didn't recognize. "A camera! Thank you!" James immediately sat down on the dock, took everything out of the box, and began to read the instructions. I was eager to see the camera, so I sat down next to James. We figured out how to load the film.

Everyone else went up to the house for cake, but we wanted to play with the camera.

"Let's take some pictures," I suggested. I held the box up to my eye.

"That's not how you do it," said James. "You hold it at your waist and look into this window, then push the button." That felt odd. We went to the barn. We each shot some photos of the lighthouse. James took one of Sarah holding Sven. Gulliver was my subject.

James soon got bored with the camera and went fishing. Excited to have a camera again, I kept looking for pictures to take. Nels said as long as James didn't want to take photos, he would appreciate it if I did. I caught a good one of Ingrid and Nels laughing on the porch and holding their coffee cups. I stood behind a tree and took one of Nellie lazing in a hammock, reading *Pride and Prejudice.* Maggie followed me around and kept trying to walk into each photo at the crucial moment. "How do you know the exact second to wreck a photo?" I said. Maggie seemed pleased with her ability.

Ingrid called to me to have cake. I joined the group. Sven was telling tales about ghosts and cursed ships, and I listened in delight for the rest of the afternoon. I asked Sven the distance to town. He said seven miles. I felt a creepy sense of aloneness, of being shipwrecked on an island. I shivered.

About supper, Sven and Joe said they had to leave. We walked down to the dock and waved good-bye. As we returned to the house, Ingrid lagged behind. When I joined her, I noticed her flushed cheeks but thought it was from all of the excitement.

What a great day! I put the camera and *Oliver Twist* on the nightstand. *I will keep taking photos as long as James doesn't want the camera.* I patted the bed for Maggie to jump up. As I fell asleep, Maggie turned onto her back, four paws in the air, and began to snore.

CHAPTER 18:

A Crisis of Magnificent Proportions

THE NEXT MORNING, NELS SHOOK me awake early. I sat up, startled.

"What's wrong?"

"Ingrid's very ill. She has a high fever, and I can't get it down. If she's not better by dawn, I'm going to have to row her into town to the doctor," he said. "We should be back by dark to light the lighthouse. Could you take care of the children until I get back?"

"Of course. But don't you have any medicine?"

He shook his head.

I wondered if this was the dire circumstance Mr. Thompson mentioned. *How can I help? I'm not a doctor.*

"What do you think she has?"

"I don't know, but I've never seen her this sick before."

"Do you have any ibuprofen?" I asked. "That's what we take when we have a fever."

"Never heard of it."

"What about aspirin?"

"I don't know. Ingrid usually takes care of all the doctoring."

"My mom was a nurse. When I was little and had a fever, she made me take a cold bath." I imagined trying to get this sick woman into the tiny tub. That would never work. "Why don't you get some cold cloths and spread them on her forehead and arms? I'll see if there's anything that looks like aspirin."

There wasn't. A bunch of glass jars with weird names like Dr. Johnson's Tonic dotted the cupboard. I wrinkled my nose. *Medicine is easier in my time.*

I got a cold cloth and went to Ingrid's room. She was burning up. I put the cloth on her forehead.

Nels patted my hand. "Thank you. I don't know what we'd do without you." This gave me a pang in the stomach, since he seemed to forget I didn't belong there. But it was nice that someone didn't think I was a complete idiot.

They left as soon as it was light. Nels carried Ingrid to the boat. He propped her up with pillows and tucked her in with a blanket. Then he rowed away.

This left me the grim task of telling everyone. Nellie slammed the door to her room, Sarah cried, and James stormed to the barn.

I thought we should keep busy. First I cooked and we ate breakfast. James managed to come back when it was ready. He was talented that way.

Next we wrote a list of all the chores. Everyone chimed in: do the dishes, make lunch, feed the horse, check the lighthouse, make dinner, feed the dog, wash the laundry, milk the cow … The list was rather daunting, but I love organizing tasks.

Then we numbered the chores. "James, do you want to clean the horse stall and Nellie and I will do the dishes?" Everyone silently went along with this plan. They cleared the table and pumped water into the sink. I washed and Nellie dried. Every once in a while Sarah would dry a dish and then resume playing under the table.

"I like helping," she said.

Nellie and I didn't say a word to each other. Against my will, I felt a wave of sympathy for her. I knew how upsetting it was to have a sick mother.

When we finished the dishes, we took Sarah with us out to the barn. We helped James finish cleaning up. Then we checked on the lighthouse. The girls swept the floors, and James helped me clean the windows and the light. Already, it was time for lunch.

CHAPTER 19:

I'm Not Going to Be a Chef

EVERYONE PROWLED AROUND THE KITCHEN. I wished for a microwave.

"How many eggs did we collect today?" I asked.

"Ten," said Sarah. "I counted them."

"We'll make an omelet," I said.

"What's an omelet?" asked Sarah.

"It's yummy," I said. "We need eggs, milk, and ingredients to put in the middle. What do we have picked from the garden?"

"We have tomatoes and green onions," James said.

"Great. Could you please get some of each?" James sauntered out the door, and it slammed behind him. "Now, do we have any chicken in the freezer?"

"What's a freezer?" asked Sarah.

"Never mind." *Didn't they have anything?* "I forgot you don't have them yet."

"We have chickens," said Nellie. "But you'd have to kill one. Mother does it by a quick wrench of the neck." Nellie demonstrated by twisting her hands together and then dropping her head.

Sarah screamed and smacked Nellie.

James walked in with the tomatoes and onions. "Or you could do it like my grandma. She put a pipe over the chicken's neck and pulled the legs, and then the head popped off and the chicken ran around the yard headless." Then he grinned wickedly and tilted his head like he always did.

Sarah shrieked.

"James, you're scaring your sister. That sounds horrible." I shuddered. "I don't think I could kill a chicken."

"Sarah, quit makin' all that racket," yelled James. Sarah clamped her mouth shut. But she punched James in the arm.

Hoping to change the subject, I asked, "Do you have any bacon?"

"Yes. There's some in the cellar," said Nellie.

"Can you go get some?"

"I'm not going alone. It's dark and there's spiders."

"I'll go with her," offered James.

We finally got all the ingredients together. James put more wood in the stove and got out the big, cast-iron skillet. I showed them how to beat the eggs and add the ingredients.

With fresh milk, bread left over from the day before, jam, and the omelet, we had a delicious lunch. But after the dishes, we had a whole afternoon to get through.

"What should we do now?" I asked. "My gran says if you stay busy, it helps keep you from worrying."

"You said that already. I'm sick of hearing about your old granny," said Nellie, rolling her eyes. "She must be ancient."

Nellie was trying to get under my skin. Since I was supposed to be the one in charge, I asked, "What year were you born?"

Nellie said 1901. James said 1900. Sarah said she didn't know.

"My grandma was born in the 1940s. She's a lot younger than you."

Nellie said, "Harrumph," and stalked off.

James grinned. "That was a good one." Then his smile faded. "She gets bossy when she's worried."

I nodded. "What should we do?"

We headed to the barn. I took the first turn riding Gulliver.

"I didn't fall off this time," I yelled, as I slid off the saddle and jumped to the ground. We led Sarah around on Gulliver. Nellie appeared, sitting on a rock.

James whispered to me, "Look who's here. Ask her if she wants a ride. Or she'll sit there all day like a goose on an egg."

"Do you want to ride?" I shouted. Nellie nodded and jumped off the rock and sidled over.

She walked along Gulliver's side and started to put her hands on the saddle, preparing to mount. Then she pulled her hands back. "Where's the side saddle?"

I was silent. I didn't feel like getting a lecture about the impropriety of riding on a regular saddle. James looked at me with mischief in his eyes.

"Paige here doesn't believe in them."

"Really?" said Nellie, who turned around to face me with her hands on her hips.

Oh, here it comes. "I don't know how to ride that way," I said. Then I felt a surge of defiance. "Plus I think they're very stupid."

Nellie stared at me in shock. And then she laughed. "Me, too. I'd like to see James ride with both feet on one side."

"No, thank you. It looks very uncomfortable."

"It is," said Nellie. "Give me a boost." James gave her a leg up, and she swung up over the saddle.

"You did that much more gracefully than I did," I said.

"Long skirts, I've worn them all my life, so I'm used to it. Giddy up," Nellie said to the horse. He trotted nicely for her around the yard. "I like this," Nellie yelled and slipped into a canter.

"See, she's not so bad when you get to know her," James said.

I nodded.

James rode Gulliver next. "I'm going to show you some jumps. I'm good, you know."

Nellie and I glanced at each other and tried not to laugh.

He got up on Gulliver by himself without a boost. He grabbed the reins and the two were off. They jumped a short bush. James jumped every bush, log, and fence possible. He halted right in front of us and patted the horse. "Good boy," he said. "Pretty good, huh?"

I laughed. "Yeah, pretty good."

When we finally had enough riding, we groomed the horse and fed and watered the animals. James milked the cow, and Sarah chased the cat. Then we all walked back to the kitchen. We were starving.

Everyone was looking at me expectantly, even the dogs. I wanted to yell that I was only twelve and hungry, too.

"Mommy always makes us biscuits," said Sarah.

"I don't know how to make biscuits from scratch," I said, tears edging up.

"What's 'from scratch'?" asked James.

"It means without someone telling you how to do it." I was too tired to explain cake mixes and frozen food. "I need some help. Someone set the table, someone pour the milk, and someone slice the bread," I commanded.

James looked in the cupboard. "There is no bread."

Of course there wouldn't be. Ingrid had been sick. I was overwhelmed. I wasn't a chef. I didn't think I could do all this without Ingrid.

Sarah tugged on my skirt. "I miss Mommy."

"I know, honey." I smoothed her hair. *What am I bellyaching for?* I took a deep breath. "Okay, no bread. What else do we have?"

"Apple pie left," said James.

"Okay, we'll have eggs and apple pie," I decided. "It will be our new invention."

That's what we had for supper. It lacked some nutritional value, but it was my best idea.

After dinner, we went to the lighthouse to get it ready for lighting. Everything seemed to be in perfect order.

James looked out at the lake. "Storm's comin'," he said.

Butterflies fluttered in my stomach. "How do you know?" I asked.

"It smells like it," explained James.

"You don't know. Let's go back to the house." I herded them out of the lighthouse.

We spent the evening playing cards and checkers. Then I read to them. I looked out the window for Nels and Ingrid, and also to see if James was right about the storm. Clouds rolled in and the wind whipped up.

"Told ya," James said into my ear.

"Yes, and unfortunately, it looks like you're right. Is there anything we need to do in the house to get ready for a storm?" A raindrop splattered on the window.

"Close all the windows," said James.

"This house must have about twenty windows," I groaned.

"Twenty-three actually," said James, grinning.

"Can you help me?" I asked Nellie.

"Sure." Together, we got all the windows closed. They were all wooden and heavy, and some were propped up with sticks. It started to rain in earnest.

I was worried. Nels wasn't back yet. *Is Ingrid okay? I hope they are safe and not caught in the storm on the lake.*

Chapter 20:

A Long Night

Rain slashed at the windows. Nels and Ingrid wouldn't be back tonight. No way of communicating with them existed: no radio, e-mail, or cell phone. We were all alone.

"I don't want to spend the night at the lighthouse by myself during a storm," I said.

"I think we should all stay together," said James.

"Maybe we should all sleep in the lighthouse," suggested Nellie.

"Good idea. It'll be like a slumber party."

"What's a lumber party?" asked Sarah.

"It's where you all sleep together on the floor. Grab some pillows and blankets."

I wanted to get to the lighthouse as quickly as possible to light the lamps. We piled everything by the back door. I banked down the fire in the stove. "James, I hope you know how to build a fire in the lighthouse stove."

"I do."

"Good. Grab the blankets and let's make a run for it."

The rain soaked through our clothing. Maggie and Ralph filled the room with the smell of wet dogs.

"Okay, we need to get the lamps lit as fast as we can. Can you all help?" I pushed wet locks of hair out of my face. We filled the lamps, trimmed the wicks, and lit them after wiping the soot from the windows and polishing the reflectors.

When the kerosene lanterns were lit, I felt a great sense of relief. Now no ships would crash because of me.

We trudged back downstairs to the office. James built a fire in the stove while the girls laid the blankets and pillows on the floor. We sat down to eat the rest of the pie.

"Don't we have any milk?" asked Sarah.

"The cow!" I exclaimed. "We forgot to milk her!"

"How could I forget the cow?" James muttered.

I looked out the window. The rain was coming down so heavily it was hard to see past the steps. "Maybe we could just skip it."

"No, we can't," said Nellie. "If we do that, Daisy will hurt all night because she'll be so full of milk."

"Oh, bother," I said, getting up. "James, can you stay here and watch the light? I'll go milk the cow."

The girls moaned.

"You can have Ralph," I said. "I'll take Maggie."

"Ralph stinks," said Sarah. "We want to go with you."

"No. It's raining cats and dogs out there."

"Really?" Sarah looked out the window. "I don't see any."

"It's an expression. It means *a lot*."

"Oh." Sarah was disappointed.

"Maybe Nellie could read you a book," I suggested. We scoured the office but all we could find were nautical charts and the logbook. "You could read them the logbook," I said. This proposal was greeted with "No, no!"

"Maybe Nellie could make up a story," I suggested.

Nellie looked up in surprise. "I could do that."

This idea was greeted with "Yes, yes!"

"I'll check the light before I go," I said.

"I can do that," said James, lying on a blanket with his head on a pillow.

"I'm up already." I ran up the spiral steps, my rain boots echoing. One of the lamps had been blown out by the wind. *Oh boy, I think we're in for a long night.* I lit it again and hopped back down. Nellie was telling a story, and Sarah watched. I donned my wet rain slicker, grabbed a lantern, and opened the door. The wind and rain howled.

"I'll be right back," I said. "Don't go anywhere else." *That was silly. Where would they go?* With that, I plunged into the darkness. The wind kept blowing me off the path, and I couldn't see the barn. Halfway there, the rain doused the lantern.

This is scary. Just keep walking.

Maggie knew the way to the barn, even in the dark. The cow was mooing and the horse nickered, knowing it was time for dinner. I took off my raincoat and felt for the peg to hang it on. Maggie shook the rain off, getting me wetter. Then she went to chase a mouse.

"I don't know why I put on a raincoat. I'm completely soaked," I said to Daisy. I reached around, feeling for the bucket and milking stool. I knocked the bucket off the nail, making a loud crash. The cow was big so I found her quite easily. I sat down, wet skirts sticking to my legs. It was spooky in the dark. But with all the practice, I had gotten quite fast at milking and finished in about twenty minutes.

I jumped up, kicking the milk bucket and spilling half its contents.

I patted Daisy. Then I felt around for some hay and threw some to Daisy and some to Gulliver. I put my jacket back on. I picked up the milk bucket and the lantern. "Come, Maggie," I called. When I got to the lighthouse, James opened the door.

I pushed my way in and spilled more milk. "Ugh."

"You're back!" Sarah hugged me. Nellie and James looked relieved. Some confidence surged in my heart.

"Who wants some milk? Fresh from the cow."

"I do," said Sarah. "What happened to it all? Usually there's more."

"I spilled a little," I said.

James snorted. I glared at him. "Are there any cups around here?" We could find only two dirty coffee cups, so we shared and each drank some milk. We all sat on the floor.

"Do you have homemade milk in the future?" asked Sarah.

"You're not supposed to know about that," I said.

"She knows," said James.

"You came from a hundred years in the future," said Sarah. "I heard mother and father talking. Can I have your bloomers that you hide under the bed?"

"They are not underwear," I said with dignity. "It's shorts and a tank top. Everyone wears them."

"What do your undergarments look like in the future?"

I blushed because James was there.

"Sarah, you're not supposed to ask questions like that. It's not polite," Nellie said.

"Sorry," said Sarah flippantly. Then she stuck her jaw out. "I'd still like to know."

"I'll tell you later in private," I promised.

"When you go home, can I go with you? I want to get a polka-dotted corset like you have."

"Wouldn't you miss your mama?" I said.

Sarah thought for a minute. "Can't Mama go, too?"

"I don't know how to get back home," I whispered. Sarah looked sad, but I didn't want to talk about it anymore. "Right now we need to make a plan."

I outlined our goals for the evening: One, keep the light lit. Two, keep everyone safe.

"That sounds easy," said James.

I didn't think so. We debated over who would go where. We decided that I would sit up by the light and guard it. James would sit downstairs with the girls. Then we would trade.

"I'd like to help," said Nellie.

I just about fainted. "You can take a shift upstairs if you like."

Nellie nodded.

I had a small kerosene lantern to take with me, but wished I had a stronger light. Going into the tower alone during a storm was scary. There's that bravery of mine again.

"Nellie, how about telling another story?" I said.

Nellie nodded.

"Sarah, first you must get under the blankets, lie down, and get all comfortable. That's the only way to hear a story." I tucked her in and then started walking upstairs.

I was feeling shaky.

"Come, Maggie." My dog wagged her tail and followed me up. She had her usual nervous misgivings toward the top.

I tucked a blanket under my arm. When I spread it out, Maggie circled and curled up in a ball on it. "You have to make room for me, you silly girl." Maggie opened one eye and looked at me, then closed it, and went back to sleep. I sighed. "A lot of help you are." I checked the light. The lamps were still lit. The rain knocked against the glass. This night was going to last forever. I sat practically on top of Maggie, and she had to move over. I felt jumpy. The wind whistled. The darkness surrounded us.

The light spun around, the rain slashed on the windows, and Maggie snored. I heard the waves colliding with the cliff. I got up every five minutes to check on the light. I sat down again and leaned my head against the wall.

Crash! I jumped up, and Maggie started barking. Something had hit one of the windows. I held the kerosene lantern up. A small crack splintered the pane.

The glass was still together, so I sat down again. I was so tired, and I wasn't supposed to fall asleep. I wondered what time it was. This was the longest night ever.

On one of my checks, I tiptoed downstairs. Sarah had curled up in a ball on the floor, asleep. James had fallen asleep sitting up. Nellie stared into the fire. I longed to join the slumber party and go to sleep.

Instead, I hiked back upstairs. I flopped down on the blanket again. I saw a flicker out of the corner of my eye. I frowned. *Did I really see something?* I stood and hurried to the window where I had seen the flash. There it was again. A spot of light on the water.

CHAPTER 21:

A Would-Be Rescue

I RUSHED DOWN THE STAIRS.

"James, James!" I shook his shoulder. He awoke with a start.

"What are you doing?" he mumbled groggily.

"I saw a light. Out on the water. I don't know what it is. Come look."

I had to give him credit. He woke up quickly when he heard this. He bounded up the steps. Maggie had come downstairs. I turned around because she was starting to follow me back upstairs. "Maggie. Stay. Watch Sarah." Maggie curled up next to Sarah.

I hurried up the steps. Nellie and James were peering out of the windows into the storm.

"Where did you see it?" asked James.

I pointed in the direction where I saw the light. Everyone squinted into the darkness. Thunder grumbled and lightning flashed, illuminating the blackness.

Nellie grabbed her brother's arm. "I saw a boat!"

James turned to his sister. "Are you sure?"

"I'm pretty sure."

We all looked into the darkness for several minutes. Nothing was visible. All we could hear was the rain and the sound of the gears going click, click, click. James turned away. "There's nuthin out there," he said. Nellie and I continued to squint into the darkness.

"James, it's a flare!" Nellie shouted. "There's a boat in trouble!"

"What's a flare?" I asked.

"It's a signal," she explained, nicely for a change. "They're asking for help."

"What are we supposed to do?" I wondered.

James peered out the window. "Nellie, are you sure? I can't see anything."

"I'm sure," she said.

"What are we going to do?" I asked.

James's face was grim. "If Father were here, we would take the rescue boat out and get them. I don't know ..." His voice trailed off.

"He told us not to leave the light," I pointed out.

Nellie grabbed James's arm. "James, what if ... what if ... it's Mother and Father out there?" This horrible idea drove us to action.

"James, we have to save them," said Nellie.

"How would you save them exactly?" I asked.

"You bring the rescue boat alongside the wreck and then pull the people into your boat," said Nellie.

"How is that possible in this storm with the high waves?" I asked.

"It's hard," said James, doubtfully. "It takes one person to steer the boat and at least one other person to haul people into the boat. Father and I did it once. I can steer and row, but it was Father who pulled people into the boat." He looked doubtfully at Nellie and me. "I don't think either of you are strong enough to pull someone out of the water."

"I could row and steer," said Nellie. "Then you and Paige could do the lifting. We can't just let them die."

They both looked expectantly at me.

"I'll help," I said, "if you tell me what to do."

"What about Sarah?"

"Maggie and Ralph can stay with her. Maggie won't leave if I tell her to stay. Won't Sarah sleep the whole time?"

"Probably," James said. "She sleeps like a log."

"What if she wakes up and we're not here?" I ran my fingers through my hair.

"We'll have to risk it," James said. "I don't think she'll go out in the storm alone."

"If we're going, we better hurry."

Chapter 22:

We're Going

NELLIE TURNED AROUND AND STARTED down the circle of stairs followed by James and me. Three sets of oilskin raincoats hung by the door. They were adult sizes. When we got them on, we looked like little gnomes, with pointed hats and the coats stretching to the floor.

"Maggie, stay with Sarah," I commanded. Maggie barked, maybe showing her objection or possibly her acceptance. It's hard to know with dogs.

I turned my attention to James, who was gathering items together.

"What do we need to bring?"

"We need a lantern, which I hope will stay lit." James put a folding knife into his pocket. "The rest of the stuff is in the boathouse. Father keeps an emergency pack there."

Nellie opened the door, and we thrust ourselves into the storm. The lantern snuffed out. We stumbled down to the lake with rain pelting our faces.

It was difficult to see far because of the storm. The steep path to the water was coated with rain and mud. The more we hurried, the more we fell. I quit counting after the fourth time. We hit the ground like baseball players sliding into home plate. Stumbling and falling, we finally reached the boathouse. The waves hit the dock like a giant hand smacking the water.

James sprinted for the boathouse and Nellie headed to the boat. I followed her. Water swirled around the bottom of the boat. "Here, hold the side," Nellie yelled over the sound of the waves. "I'm going to try to get in." I knelt down and grabbed the side of the boat, which was up one second and down the next. The dock rocked and I stiffened, keeping my balance. I watched in admiration as Nellie hopped into the boat. Nellie grabbed a bucket and began bailing water out of the boat. She yelled at me to get in. I didn't think I could. I watched the boat go up and down and tried to gauge when I could jump. I was ready to spring when a loud bang sounded behind me. The noise startled me so much, I lost my balance and fell onto the dock. "Ouch." I struggled to get up. James came over to help me. He carried a gun.

"What is that for?" I yelled.

"It's a flare gun to let the people know we saw them and are coming." He grabbed my elbow.

"Well, you might have warned me," I shouted as I tried to get up on the slippery boards.

"Sorry. I didn't think of it."

I finally stood up.

"You better get into the boat."

I decided if I thought about it any longer, I would never have the guts to do it. I leaped off the dock and landed on my butt with a thud.

Nellie handed me a bucket. "Start bailing," she said. I took it, got onto the seat, and began scooping out the water.

Meanwhile, James prepared to get in. He undid the mooring, tossed the rope to Nellie, then jumped in. Nellie handed him the oars one at a time, and soon he was dipping them into the angry water, trying to pull the boat away from the dock.

The water seemed to have other ideas. James would row, and we would go forward a bit, but then a wave would come and wash us back again to where we had started. Finally, after getting only about five feet from the dock, James yelled, "Nellie, help me. Come and row!"

Nellie crawled across the boat and sat next to James. He took the right oar, she took the left, and they rowed in unison. I bailed. Every wave pushed water over the edge of the boat, and the water sloshed around the bottom.

Nellie and James struggled to coordinate their rowing. James was stronger than Nellie, and at first, when they rowed, they went in a circle to the right. This put us parallel to the waves, which started rolling into the boat. Soon we were drenched, and the boat sank lower in the water.

"Nellie, row as hard as you can!" After many attempts, they brought the boat around perpendicular to the waves and headed out to the lake once more. I speeded up the bailing. I was wet from head to toe. So this was what forty-degree water felt like. The rain stung my face. My shoulder cramped from bailing. I stopped to watch James and Nellie.

James matched his rowing to Nellie's, and they made some progress forward, still perpendicular to the waves. "Don't stop bailing!" shouted James. I resumed bailing, wishing I were anywhere but in this boat on the lake.

In the dark, I couldn't tell if we were making headway. James had said he knew where we were going, but I couldn't see beyond the edges of the boat. The rain and darkness blinded me. Every few seconds, the lighthouse lamp would sweep over our heads, briefly illuminating the night. I was freezing. How could we find a boat in the dark? Someone out there needed help. I kept scooping water out of the boat and throwing it over the side. Blisters coated my palms.

James and Nellie slowed down, apparently from exhaustion, their faces strained and white. The waves kept pushing them backward.

A deep weariness came over me. *Why did I come? I don't know anything about handling a boat. I should have stayed at the lighthouse. I am no good at all.*

Tears dropped from my eyes and mixed with the rain. This ticked me off. I hate crying.

I stopped bailing and looked out onto the lake. Lightning flashed. In the brief light, I saw the boat. I poked James in the knee. "I saw it!" I yelled.

"What?" said James.

"The boat!"

James turned around. "I can't see anything."

"Row straight ahead!"

James told Nellie, and they began rowing with renewed vigor. It took another fifteen minutes of rowing and bailing to get to where we could see the boat. Could it be Ingrid and Nels? The overturned rowboat with two people sitting on it looked precarious. Every wave threatened to pull them off and dunk them into the angry water. I knew from stories that once dumped into the lake, people drowned quickly. I also knew that shipwrecked people hanging onto wreckage could get hypothermia. As their limbs froze up, they would lose their grasp. I pushed aside how cold and wet and miserable I was.

CHAPTER 23:

Misery Has Company

As we got closer, Nellie yelled, "It's not them! It's not Ma and Pa! It's a boy and a man!"

"Thank God." My relief felt like pin prickles.

We could finally see the outline of a man holding a little boy, one arm clasped tightly around the boy's chest and the other arm holding onto the boat's rope.

I hadn't a clue what we were going to do now that we were here. "What now?" I shouted at James. He didn't answer. It looked like he was trying to bring our boat alongside the upturned one. I didn't see how we were going to do it without crashing into the other boat. I stopped bailing to watch.

James steered us near to the boat. Nellie rowed us forward with one oar. I wished I could do something.

As James rowed closer to the overturned boat, a wave would come and part us again. I admired James and Nellie. They didn't give up. I counted the times they brought our boat near the other boat. Five times the waves washed us apart.

On the sixth try, they maneuvered near enough for Nellie to toss a rope. The man grabbed for it with one hand, the other hand clutching the boy. He missed, and the rope cascaded into the waves. Nellie wound it back up while the waves parted us.

James brought us close to the boat. Nellie tossed the line, and this time the man caught it. He tied the rope beneath the boy's arms. The boy had some kind of life jacket on, though it was strange-looking to me.

Then I witnessed a brave act. The man gently lowered the boy into the water. The boy hadn't moved. The life jacket kept him afloat. Nellie started to pull the rope toward us.

"He's too heavy! I need help!" Nellie yelled.

I grabbed the wet rope above Nellie's hands and yanked. The waves pulled against us. The boy and the boats continued to bob up and down. Nellie and I pulled in a life-or-death tug of war. I gave all of my strength, the skin ripping off my palms.

At first it seemed the boy wasn't moving any closer. But slowly we made progress. My arms ached from the strain and the cold. With one last yank, we brought the boy next to the boat.

"Grab under his arms," shouted James. We each grabbed the boy. He was not as heavy as we thought, and we tumbled backward as we lifted the boy out of the water and slid him into the boat. He landed on top of us. We carefully lifted him up and propped him against the side of the boat.

I looked at his pale face. I could tell he was only about five years old. His eyes were closed. I put my ear to his chest and felt his heart still beating. Nausea gripped me. I realized he could die.

Nellie brought me back to practical things. "Help me untie this rope." Wet fibers tightened the knot. We struggled for several minutes but couldn't budge it.

"James, we can't get it," I said.

"Leave it. I brought another rope," James yelled, still steering with one hand and pointing with the other. Nellie scrambled to get the other rope. I kept looking at the boy. I wished I had something to wrap around him, but everything in the boat was soggy.

Nellie tossed the second rope to the man. It fell a foot short. She shouted at James, "You're going to have to get closer!" Her brother steered nearer to the boat.

Nellie threw the rope again. This time it was long enough, but the man reached out, lost his balance, and tumbled headfirst into the water.

"Oh no!" I wailed. The man's head popped up out of the water, but he didn't have a life jacket and he kept going under.

CHAPTER 24:

A Dive

I GRABBED MY BOOTS AND pulled them off. I yanked at my wet skirt until it came off.

Nellie grabbed my arm. "What are you doing?"

"I'm going to get him."

"You can't go in there. You'll drown!"

James said, "I better go."

I felt sure that this was what I needed to do. "I'm the best swimmer. I should go." There was silence. They knew it was true.

James grimaced. "Take a rope."

I secured the rope around my waist. I looked out to locate the man. His head went under just as I jumped in the lake.

The shock of the cold water took my breath away. I surfaced as soon as I could, gasping for air. The angry water tore at me, trying to pull me under.

I peered around, looking for the man as the waves kept rolling over my head. His head popped up again. I started swimming toward him but couldn't feel my limbs. I couldn't get nearer to him. This made me mad. I gritted my teeth. I wasn't going to let him drown right in front of me. My expert arm stroked through the waves and I coaxed my frozen legs to kick.

Finally, I got closer. The man fixed his gaze on me now and I could see his blue, bloodshot eyes. A massive wave washed over us and I sucked in a bunch of water. I kicked my way to the surface, then coughed while treading water to stay upright. I looked around.

The man had vanished!

With swift strokes, I reached the spot where he had bobbed. I grabbed around in the water with my hands. Nothing. I dove under the dark water and swam in a circle, reaching out, hoping to feel some clothing and yank him up. Nothing.

On the second circle, I dove deeper and my hand touched some cloth. I snatched it and pulled. I was sure it was the man because the bundle of clothes weighed a ton. I found an arm and kicked with all my might. An eternity passed before we reached the surface. He coughed a lot but at least he was breathing. I shifted my arm underneath the man's arms so his head stayed above water. Now that I had him, I didn't know how we were going to get to the boat because I was exhausted. I yanked on the rope and yelled.

I felt a tug on the rope. I couldn't use my arms while holding onto the man, but I could kick. *I'll be hanged if we're going to drown now!*

It seemed forever, but finally Nellie and James pulled us to the edge of the boat. No one paddled or steered.

A new problem emerged. How would we get the man into the boat? He was bigger than any of us, and although he was conscious, he wouldn't be much help. Nellie and James each tried tugging one of his arms, but he was too heavy.

"Hang onto him and I'll get in!" I tried to pull myself up, but my cold and tired arms prevented it and I fell back into the water. I attempted again, and this time managed to get one arm over the edge of the boat. James held on to the man, and Nellie grabbed my arm and pulled. I was able to inch my way up to my waist and then I tumbled into the boat headfirst.

I scrambled to Nellie and James. The boat tipped from all the weight on one side. Nellie and I grabbed one of the man's arms and James took the other. "One, two, three—pull!" We all yanked. The man landed halfway in the boat, his legs still in the water.

A big wave crashed over us, but we held on tightly and the man fell only a short distance back into the lake.

"One, two, three—pull!" I pulled with every cell in my body. The man came into the boat face first. Success!

"We'd better get back before we freeze to death," said James. This was a real possibility. We were all so cold our teeth were chattering. James took up one of the oars. Nellie grabbed the other and they rowed. This left me in charge of the patients. The man was sitting on the bottom of the boat with his eyes closed. The boy was next to him. Though he was bone-tired, the man had managed to put his arm around the boy. This made me teary-eyed. No one had spoken. The only words the man had said were to ask if the boy was all right. I had assured him he was, in spite of a nasty cut on his forehead.

As we crept closer to the shore, I began gathering in my head everything I knew about first aid. *Get everyone warm as soon as possible.* My brave self also took this opportunity to throw up over the side of the boat. It might have been all that water I swallowed or it might have been because I'd been scared out of my wits.

The storm subsided, and we made it to the dock in record time.

CHAPTER 25:

Warm Blankets, Hot Coffee

RUBBER LEGS. SWIMMING AND THE cold water created wobbly legs. I almost fell when I got out of the boat, but steadied myself. I helped the other people exit. Luckily, the boy awoke; he could walk with help. Otherwise, I don't know how we would have made it up the hill to the lighthouse.

We moored the boat and headed up the hill. James helped the little boy, who was having a hard time walking. The man walked between Nellie and me, his hands resting on our shoulders. Our arms encircled his waist. Everyone shivered.

The climb to the lighthouse took a long time. We tumbled in the door and made a beeline for the fire. Sarah was still fast asleep, cuddled in a warm ball, but Maggie and Ralph looked up.

"I'll go to the house and grab a bunch of clean clothes," I said. "Nellie, could you make some hot coffee?"

Nellie nodded.

"James, could you rig up a dressing room so everyone could get out of their wet clothes?"

James said yes.

The man and the boy sat before the fire in a stupor.

I crept into the dark house with a lantern. I raided everyone's room, grabbing pants and shirts, dresses, and socks. I also grabbed some blankets.

No one spoke as we went about the business of getting everyone changed. James had to help the man and the boy. When they had on dry clothes, I sat them in front of the stove with a blanket and a cup of hot coffee. They still hadn't said more than thanks. I washed off the cut on the boy's head. After they drank their coffee, they leaned over and fell asleep.

My turn to change came last. I had already taken off my shoes in the boat, so I had on only my torn stockings. I ripped off those soggy things, then stood on one leg so I could examine the bottoms of my feet. Cuts and scrapes etched them from toe to heel. The rope took a layer of skin from my palms.

I put on a dry dress of Ingrid's. My numb fingers didn't want to button. I threw one of Nels's keeper coats over the dress because I was so cold, then added his socks with no shoes. I walked on tiptoe out of the dressing room because it hurt less.

Nellie and James displayed quite an array of clothing. Nellie wore James's overalls because I couldn't find any clean dresses. James had on some of Nels's pants, which were way too big, and a ragged flannel shirt.

When I got changed, Nellie stretched out her hand with a tin of coffee. I took the offered cup.

Once everyone wore dry clothes, snuggled in a blanket, and sipped coffee, the mood in the room lightened. I ripped up a sheet to wrap around my hands, which made them feel much better. Nellie and James's skin bled, and I wrapped their hands, too.

James checked the light and filled up the kerosene lamps. It stopped raining. We sat on our blankets, not talking. One by one, we fell asleep.

CHAPTER 26:

It's Over

I AWOKE AND SAT UP. *What happened?* Wet with sweat, I pushed my damp bangs out of my eyes. The lake turned to millions of hands, reaching to grab me, and voices cried for me to save them. I hadn't been able to help any of them. *Horrible.* But I realized it was a nightmare.

We rescued them. Still, it didn't seem real. I crept out of my quilt onto the cold floor. I tiptoed over to where the boy and the man slept. I could see their outlines in the dark, and I could hear their breathing. The man snored. This made me smile.

They're all right. They're here because I helped save them. Then I crept back to my blanket, wrapped myself up, and went back to sleep.

I awoke later and ran up the stairs to check on the light. The wicks still lit, the kerosene burned as the lanterns shot their warning light to sailors. A faint gray line separated the lake from the sky. The long night neared its end. I watched the sun until it was a complete circle in the sky. Then I extinguished the lanterns and ran down the stairs.

Nellie and Sarah looked like two cocoons. The man and the boy looked pale, but they were sleeping peacefully. James was up, stoking the fire.

"Want coffee?" he whispered. He handed me a tin.

"Thanks," I said and cradled it in my palms.

"Are you all right?" I asked. "You look pale."

"You don't look so great yourself," he snapped. "You have dirt all over, your hair's a mess, and you smell like vomit."

This struck me as funny. I tried to laugh quietly since people were sleeping, which is difficult if you've ever tried to do it. It didn't work. I laughed until the tears rolled down my face.

Pretty soon, James grinned. "Now you have stripes on your face," he said.

Sarah and Nellie sat up, their hair all tussled, Nellie's still damp.

"What's so funny?" demanded Nellie.

I finally stopped laughing. "We just made it through the night. That's all I care about."

"What's there to eat?" asked Sarah, getting to the important stuff.

The boy and the man remained asleep.

The rest of us decided to move to the house and make eggs. We shuffled out the door into the crisp air. We headed to the barn to milk the cow and collect the eggs when we saw a sight that shocked us all: Nels walking toward us, carrying Ingrid.

"Mama!" the girls screamed and ran toward her. James sprinted off, too. Nels put Ingrid gently down on the steps of the house. Ingrid looked much better. The children hugged their parents tightly. Then they all began to talk at once and no one could hear anyone.

I stayed behind, feeling like an intruder.

Ingrid looked at me. She waved at me to come.

I picked up my skirts and ran to Ingrid and Nels. I gave them the biggest hug I had in me. "I'm so glad you're all right. I was so worried that you got caught on the lake in that tiny little boat ..."

"Father, we kept the light going and there's a strange man sleeping in the lighthouse ..." Sarah said.

"I'm a little confused about what happened ..." Ingrid began.

"We had to take the boat out ..." Nellie interrupted.

Nels smiled. "Well, I'm just glad you're safe."

"Let's go inside, shall we?" Ingrid said. "Then you can tell us all about it."

CHAPTER 27:

Shall I Go or Shall I Stay?

THE NEXT DAY, WE SAT in the parlor, having tea. The man and the boy turned out to be Hans and Jimmy. Nels tended to their cuts and bruises, since Ingrid was weak, and they wore clothes belonging to Nels and James, since their only clothes needed washing and mending.

I relaxed on the fainting couch, my shoulders sore. My calves ached from kicking, and my palms stung from where the skin had been ripped off by the ropes.

I felt overwhelmed with all that had happened. I wanted time alone. I excused myself and went to say hi to Gulliver. As I walked toward the barn, a man slid out of the sky. He did a summersault as he landed, but his top hat stayed on.

"Mr. Thompson! I thought you were a dream."

He took off his hat and bowed. "Doing fine, thank you. Very much alive. Excellent mission." He reached out, took my hand, and kissed it. No one had ever done that before.

I couldn't think of anything to say. Then I did. "What are you doing here?"

He said nothing.

It struck me. "You're here to take me home, aren't you?" The thought filled me with sadness.

"Yes, your escort home."

"I don't know if I'm ready to go."

"Yes, feel that way. Love them. Your family. The Christiansens."

I crossed my arms. "I'm not going," I announced.

Mr. Thompson didn't say anything.

"They love me, and I like it here. I'm staying." I clamped my jaw shut. Still, Mr. Thompson stayed silent, just looking at me.

"They hate me … you know … my family." Once it was out, I couldn't believe I had said it.

He nodded in agreement. "Not nice to you."

I was shocked at someone else speaking so openly. "People said I was making it up."

Mr. Thompson twirled his hat. "No. Great evil there. But nothing to do with you."

"So I live in the wrong place at the wrong time." Bitterness coated each word, and I felt hatred flicker in my heart.

"Don't hate. Can't see everything. Whys are hidden." His voice softened. "Grieve the losses. Remember your gifts. Love. Stubbornness. Curiosity. Adaptability. Time travel." He grinned. He had huge teeth. "Now horse-riding. Or horse-falling."

I didn't see the humor. "If they hate me, why can't I just stay here? This could be my family now. Why do I have to go?"

Mr. Thompson twirled his hat in the opposite direction. "Could stay, of course," he said slowly. "Ramifications."

"Like what?"

"Stuck forever. Irreversible. No other assignments. That would be a blow. Many trips in the future."

I discounted the last sentence, but was interested in the other parts. "What was my assignment here?"

"Loving the family. Learning to work together. Learning to adjust. Helping rescue people. Letting people love you."

"Are they really important people in the future?"

"Everyone is." Mr. Thompson kept twirling his hat. It was getting on my nerves.

"Everyone is what?"

"Important. Everyone."

"Like does the boy become president or save the world and that's why he couldn't die?"

"Doubt it. Just ordinary and needed saving."

"But what happens to them?"

"I have no idea." Mr. Thompson pulled the sleeve of his topcoat over his ragged cuff.

"But is he important somehow?"

Mr. Thompson stopped fiddling with his clothes. He looked me in the eyes. "Told you. Everyone is. They all are. Important. Every last one."

I didn't get it, but I let it go.

"Your choice. Go or stay."

"Can I have time to think about it?"

"Yes. We're not using up time in the future. Heh, heh. Little time travel humor."

I didn't laugh. Without warning, Mr. Thompson did a flip and disappeared bit by bit.

"Where are you going?"

The voice sounded like it was coming from a tunnel. "Something off-world ..." With a pop, his hat disappeared.

CHAPTER 28:

The Big Decision

I STOOD THERE FOR A minute, wondering what to do. I thought about going to the lighthouse, but the barn was a good place to think.

Gulliver nickered when I approached. I grabbed a grooming brush and ducked under the door chain.

I brushed him for a while, avoiding thoughts of Mr. Thompson and home. I realized I loved it here. I loved the lighthouse and the barn. I loved my new family, even sort of liked Nellie. No one except my gran and my real mother had ever loved me like the Christiansens. It was like getting more air when you didn't know you had been gasping for breath.

I had brushed one side of Gulliver and now was trying to finger-comb the hay out of his tail. He kept flipping it out of my hands, making me laugh.

"Quit being naughty." It was a game we played. He would stop for a moment and then start again. Then I would grab his tail again and keep combing until he pulled it loose again.

Should I give up time traveling? Pictures formed of the places I would like to visit: ancient Egypt, medieval Europe, the colonial United States, maybe even the future. Mr. Thompson had said something about going off-world. Were there other planets? That sounded amazing and impossible!

I went back and forth like a teeter-totter all day.

CHAPTER 29:

Plenty of Time

IN THE END, I DECIDED to go back. I hated to do it—return to the same hardened stepmother, the turtle father who rarely came out, and the evil brothers. And leave the keeper and his family behind. But getting to time travel more in the future, that dream surpassed everything else. I wanted to see life in other time periods, in other places. I was going to be a time traveler!

"Am I allowed to say good-bye?" I asked.

"Plenty of time. Ha, ha," joked Mr. Thompson.

I said good-bye to Daisy and Gulliver first. Mr. Thompson produced an apple from his voluminous coat. Gulliver's huge teeth clamped down, and the whole treat disappeared in one gulp.

We walked slowly toward the house.

"Will I ever see the family again?" I asked.

"Doubt it," said Mr. Thompson gently.

I stopped walking and started crying. Mr. Thompson patted my back and gave me his enormous red handkerchief.

"Clean," he said. "A spare." I dried my tears.

We walked quietly into the kitchen. Everyone was in the parlor, talking and laughing. Hans and Jimmy were there, too, and the dogs. They all stopped and looked at me when I came in. Tears threatened again.

"You're just in time for cookies," said James.

Ingrid looked at me. "I don't think Paige will be joining us."

Nels stared at Mr. Thompson, who bowed.

I shook my head no. My voice wouldn't come out.

"Where is she going, Mama?" asked Sarah.

"She's going back to her father and mother," said Ingrid.

"But I want her to stay here!" yelled Sarah, and ran to hug me around my knees. Everyone got up one by one from the table to say good-bye. Hans thanked me again and again for saving them. Nellie hugged me. (I was so shocked I almost forgot to hug her back.) James solemnly shook my hand. Ingrid gave me a hug and whispered in my ear, "Thanks for taking care of my babies for me. I shall miss you dearly." I hugged her back without saying anything. My voice had disappeared.

Nels came over. "Will you be popping into my lighthouse again?" He glanced at me and then at Mr. Thompson. I looked at the floor. Mr. Thompson shook his head slightly.

"That's too bad," Nels said. "It was exciting." He smiled. Then he became serious. "I will miss you. You were the best assistant I ever had. You kept the light going in a terrible situation. I am proud of you." Nels reached up and took his hat off the peg. "I'd like you to have my lightkeeper's hat. You've earned it."

I took the hat. Tears stung my eyes. I managed to croak, "Thank you all. I shall miss you terribly."

I bolted out the door, followed by Maggie and Mr. Thompson.

We heard the door slam and there was James, running toward me. He kissed me on the cheek and ran back into the house. Mr. Thompson said I blushed, but I'm sure he was wrong. He can't be right about everything.

We stood looking at the sun on the lake. "Now what?" I asked, holding tightly onto Maggie's collar. "Do we touch the journal?"

Once again, Mr. Thompson grabbed my hand and a large black hole opened in the ground. We stepped into it. I held on to Mr. Thompson tightly with one hand and Maggie with the other. It seemed like we fell forever.

We landed with a thud on a wooden floor.

"Nice landing."

I looked around. "Where are we?"

"Recognize it?"

It took me a minute, but we were in the parlor of the lightkeeper's house.

"When is this?" I asked.

Mr. Thompson looked at his watch. "Back at closing time the day you left."

We heard voices in the hall. "I best be going," Mr. Thompson said, lifting his hat. "We'll meet again."

With that, his top hat began to fall to the ground. As it did, Mr. Thompson evaporated section by section. The hat went down over his head, which disappeared. Then over his chest, then over his legs. Finally, just his feet were poking out from underneath the hat. The toes wiggled and turned to mist, and the hat spun around on its brim. When it came to a stop, the top hat melted into the floor and was gone.

"Well," I said. Maggie barked and wagged her tail. I felt like I needed to sit down. I started to sit on the fainting couch. I noticed I had my shorts and tank top on again.

One of the modern-day guides entered the room.

"You can't sit there," she scolded. "These are museum pieces."

I was dazed. "Museum pieces?"

"Of course. They're a hundred years old."

Confusion enveloped me. "Oh, yeah, I forgot."

"Also, get that dog out of here."

"Yes, ma'am," I said. I grabbed Maggie's collar and headed out the back door.

"No, you can't go out that way. You have to go out the front door."

That really hit me. This had been my home and now it wasn't. I wandered out the front door and onto the lawn. I stood there, holding Maggie. I couldn't seem to think of what to do next. I looked around. I did have the sense to wrap the lightkeeper's hat in my warm-up jacket so no one would think I stole it.

I saw my parents steaming toward me like a freight train.

"Where have you been?" my stepmom barked. "You were supposed to meet us half an hour ago. Now we're going to be late for dinner."

I was extremely tired. I didn't know if I could make it to the car. "Sorry. I lost track of time."

"Let's get going," she snapped. We headed for the car, Maggie by my side.

Twin brother one grabbed the keeper's hat from my hand. "Where'd you get the cool hat?" He tossed it to twin brother two. He dropped it on the ground. I picked it up. I knew that my family would be the same, but it still hurt.

We started to walk through the visitor center to the parking lot. I glanced at some of the photos of the lighthouse. On the wall was a formal portrait of the Christiansen family. It stabbed my heart to see it.

"I'll meet you outside," I said to brother one.

"Could I buy a copy of that picture on the wall?" I asked the clerk in the visitor center.

"Sure. I have it in this book." The clerk pulled the book down for me and showed me where the photo was. I slammed the book shut to avoid crying. "I'll take it."

I ran to the car and got in, hardly listening to the tongue-lashing while I looked at the picture of my lighthouse family. Blessedly, I soon fell asleep, missed dinner, and just like when I time-traveled to the lighthouse, slept soundly for twenty-four hours straight. My parents left me in the car until I woke up.

CHAPTER 30:

Adjustments

When I woke up, I felt much better. I climbed out of the car and bolted to my room. I loved my room. No one bothered me there. I grabbed some clean shorts and a T-shirt and headed for the bathroom. The hot water pounding on my back felt luxurious. I hadn't had a shower in months. The dirt and stink were real. I stayed until I ran out of hot water.

I got dressed and looked in the mirror doubtfully. My shorts and T-shirt were smaller than my Edwardian underwear. I felt kinda "neck-ed," as Nels would say, compared with the way I felt in my long skirts. I reminded myself that I was back in the twenty-first century and many of my friends would be wearing less. Still, it felt as odd as when I first put on 1910 clothes.

I left my long hair down to dry. That felt weird, too, after wearing it up for so long. While chewing a peanut-butter- and-jelly sandwich, I went to my computer. I wanted to look up the accounts of the boat rescue. I logged onto the historical society Web site and downloaded the lighthouse keeper's logs. There, in Ingrid's handwriting, the entry for August 16, 1910, said, "Our friend Paige, without thought of her own life, helped save two people after a boat capsized in a storm. Without Paige, they would have died. She received this special commendation from the organization of lighthouse keepers. Since it arrived after she left, we traced a copy of it here in hopes that she might see it someday." My eyes filled with tears and I couldn't read any more.

I traced the round shape of the commendation with my forefinger. I then went to the Jagged Rock photo archives. I found a photo of Nels standing stiffly in his uniform in front of the lighthouse. Then I found one of the family, playing catch out in the yard. There was one of laundry day, one of Sarah playing with Ralph, James in his boat, Nellie on Gulliver, Ingrid churning butter.

These photos are really good, I thought. *I wonder who took them.* I looked for a credit line. "Photos by Paige Johnson, 1910." I was astounded. I had forgotten that my pictures taken with James's camera hadn't been developed when I left. I had never seen them. And here they were, better than I ever hoped. I wept then for what I had lost, and this time I didn't care that I was crying.

When I stopped crying, I printed the article, the photos, and the drawing and put them in my journal. I still had tears in my eyes when my computer sang out, "You've got mail." I snuffled, wiped my nose on my T-shirt, and checked my inbox. I had ten messages from friends welcoming me back.

My cell phone started ringing. It was Alicia, one of my best friends. The doorbell rang, Maggie began to bark, and Gran exploded into the room and engulfed me with a hug. It felt good. My grandmother doesn't talk; she booms, and she started in about what we were going to do now that I was back from vacation. In the excitement, Maggie barked so much I could hardly hear, but I caught *shopping* and *lunch* and *movie* and *cookies,* all of which sounded great. I also had a horse riding lesson (my gran paid for those), a birthday party, and a tennis match.

I laughed and hugged Gran again, drinking in her lavender scent. Mr. Thompson had promised there would be more adventures. But for now, I was back.

NANCY BAYNE VISITED TWENTY LIGHTHOUSES to research this book and read many accounts of lightkeepers and their adventures. She lives in Lincoln, Nebraska, with her husband, Tim, and her daughter, Lauren, and their chocolate Labrador, Reese, in a century-old house. Nancy, a writer for thirty years, works in communications and public relations.

Reese

CPSIA information can be obtained at www.ICGtesting.com
Printed in the USA
LVOW081036230513

335184LV00002B/89/P